TAME
THE SAVAGE
HEART

Michael Edwin Q.

TAME
THE SAVAGE
HEART

MICHAEL EDWIN Q.

Published by: ADVANTAGE BOOKS™
                  Longwood, Florida, USA
                  www.advbookstore.com

Library of Congress Catalog Number: 2019936755

1. Fiction:: African American - Woman
2. Fiction: African American – Historical
3. Social Science - Slavery

Cover Design: Alexander von Ness
Edited by: Nancy E. Sabitini

First Printing: March 2019
19 20 21 22 23 24   10 9 8 7 6 5 4 3 2 1
Printed in the United States of America

One

In Those Days

I will be dead soon. This is no great revelation; I never expected to live long enough to see the twentieth century, yet here I am well into it.

This is our story. Though I am the one telling it, it is not mine, it is ours. I get so much happiness from saying *Our Story*. There is so much joy in the words *We* and *Us*. The world has more than its share of *I, Me, Mine.*

People believe life starts when you are born and take your first breath. However, if you live with your mind and heart open, there are many times you are reborn. True life starts when you connect with someone outside yourself.

After all these years, it shines clear in my memory, as clear and bright as the sun that rose this morning, even those parts I learned from others years later.

Inwardly, I still feel like a young girl in love, only as I write this, I look down at my hands, they tell a different story, they tell the truth.

For now, put aside these images and think of me as I was, a young, black, slave girl in her teens with unblemished skin as dark as roasted coffee. My frame was slender and petite. Looking into my eyes, you would have seen innocents, for looking out of them that was all I saw, because that's what I was. The world was still young and fresh in those days.

My name is Audean. My mother once heard the mistress of the plantation tell her children a goodnight story about a princess whose name was Audean, Princess Audean. She vowed if she ever had a little girl, she would name her Princess Audean. Thankfully, my father persuaded her to give up on the princess part.

I was the oldest of three children, my sister Deidra, two years my junior, my brother Lucius two years her junior. Deidra was a beautiful child; the epitome of cute and sweet bundled tightly to form a little girl. Lucius was all boy, into anything that involved dirt and filth. Singularly, well-behaved they were, although together, they would commit misdemeanors neither one of them would have committed on their own. Deidra took after Papa with strong facial features. Lucius took after Mama, a prettiness seldom seen in boys, with eyelashes out to here.

Papa was tall, lanky, and muscular with strong, chiseled good looks. He was a fieldworker, well liked, respected by all.

Beautiful describes my mother. Even today, I can still see her angelic face speaking loving words to me. She was everything a woman could hope for and strive to be, strong, gentle, wise and caring, beautiful within and without.

Both my parents were first generation American slaves. Meaning, their parents, my grandparents, were from Africa, the old country as folks called it. Therefore, they received Old Country names, which I learned in secret, yet, heard so seldom I no longer remember them. African names were forbidden for those born on the plantation. So, they received new names, Joseph and Mary, names given them by the Master and Mistress of the plantation.

We lived and worked on the Gethen Plantation. When I say lived and worked that is only part of the story, only a half-truth, for we were more than that. We were slaves. The lives we lived were not our own, the work we did was not for our benefit. We were the property of Furcas Gethen.

There are many stories about how the Gethen family migrated from Wales, settled in the south of the United States, and started their eight hundred acre cotton plantation. All these stories have become legend, so grand that they no longer resemble anything near reality. The stuff fairytales are made of.

Furcas Gethen was in his mature years, neither too old nor too young. Sadly, there was no boy left in the man. Every man should keep a bit of boy in them. He was neither tall nor short or fat nor slim. His head was slightly square, flat on the sides. His wavy hair with enough salt and pepper to make it look steel gray, as did his closely cropped full beard. This set off his coal black eyes that only stared ahead, making it impossible to tell what he was looking at. Always dressed in high fashion made it clear he never had and never would do any menial labor. He was not a hands-on person. He would give orders, and his word would be law.

Furcas Gethen was a realist. He was neither cruel nor kind. If a slave was hungry, he'd feed them. If they were cold, he'd clothe and shelter them. If they committed an infraction, they were punished. To break the law of the plantation was a death sentence. Nothing drawn out or cruel, mind you, like a hanging, just a quick bullet to the head was all that was required, unless he felt ornery, which was most often.

His family consisted of three, his wife, Amy, and two children, Jason and Jenny, fifteen and thirteen, at the time of this story, respectively.

From what most referred to as being from a good family, Amy Gethen was lovely, a petite porcelain doll of a woman with shiny black hair and deep violet eyes. She was shy, speaking little, often with no opinions. Furcas did not love her, but he loved being married to her. She had the look and the temperament he wanted in a woman, and she gave him children. He could want no more or less.

The Gethen's children were a perfect mixture of mother and father. They had their mother's good looks and temperament. However, Furcas' cunning and aggressive selfishness was obvious to all.

As for my family and I, we lived with the other slaves in the slave quarters, a few acres of rocky, poor farmland with rows of simple shacks. Though, our home was better than most, a little larger, three rooms, better built with a wide fireplace for cooking, light, and winter heat. The reason for this blessing was my mother. She worked in the main house where the Gethen Family lived. She worked in the kitchen as the head cook. This alone was no cause for special treatment other than Furcas Gethen loved my mama's cooking. Her coffee and hoecakes started his day. Her stews made his mouth water, her fried chicken nearly brought him to tears.

Through my mother's influence, I was given the job to help her in the kitchen. There was also hope that I would grow and learn in the shadow of my mother so the next generation of the Gethen family would eat as well as the incumbent.

As for my poor brother and sister, Deidra and Lucius, they were destined to work in the fields. Their quota of work adjusted to their age and size.

Every morning, my siblings would head for the fields with our father. As for me, the eldest, I accompanied our mother to the main house for a day of cooking. I was better dressed, better fed, and better treated.

At the end of the day, we returned to our home, tired. Though as a late supper service called for us to be away longer, mother and I came home later than the others. Although, there is more than one type of *tired*, mother and I didn't come home battered and bruised, our muscles and joints aching, our clothes filthy. This caused a rift between my siblings and me. They wanted to be glad for me, that at least one of us didn't have to suffer. Only, try as they may, the green head of jealously laughed down on them, taunting them.

The main house was all one could image, the ideal Southern Mansion. It was two stories high with windows on all sides. There were four Roman style pillars at the front of the building supporting the wide overhang shading the veranda. There were twenty-six rooms in all with nearly as many fireplaces, most of them small except for the one in the dining room, the other in the sitting room.

A typical day for my mother and I started early, before sunrise. Furcas enjoyed a large breakfast, of coffee, hoecakes, eggs, and pork belly. The mistress of the house always ate little, starting her day with tea and a dry biscuit. Furcas insisted his children receive mush and a large glass of milk, a meal he felt befitting youngsters.

My mother ran her kitchen like the captain of a ship, full speed ahead. She knew all the recipes, all the secrets about how to make them the best way possible. Where and from whom did she learn these tricks of the trade I never knew. I only knew she was a good and patient teacher, teaching me all her magic.

"Ya don't throw the shells away, child," she'd say as she held the eggshells from the eggs she'd crack and put into a bowl. "Ya put the shells in the coffee as it's brewin'. They takes out the bitterness of the coffee. Just make sure ya fish them out before ya pour it." She held up the bowl in her arms. "Ya take a fork, bust the yolks, and scramble 'em. Move the fork high, so ya get a lot of air in 'em. That makes 'em fluffy. A little salt and pepper, and a splash of water, not milk!"

Another one of my mother's secrets was chicken broth. Whenever serving chicken at the main house, she'd save the bones, put them in a big pot with water, carrots, celery, and onions. There was always a pot of chicken broth warming on the back burner.

"Don't let 'em tells ya different, the chicken is the most flavorful meat there is," she'd tell me. She'd ladle a scoop of broth into nearly everything. Of course, she'd put it in chicken dishes. Other than what was expected, she put chicken broth in beef dishes, stews, roasts, as well as pork dishes. Even in recipes for wild game, pheasant, quail, deer, and rabbit.

After nearly a year working in the kitchen, learning from my mother, I was a capable cook. Not anything to sing about, but I could get by. There were even times when my mother was under the weather that I held down the kitchen on my own and no one knew the wiser.

The days flowed into one another till time meant nothing, it passed like the wind, swiftly and usually unnoticed. If not for the changing of the seasons, we never even realized time was passing. Everyday was the same. That is until the day he came to the Gethen Plantation. That is he, the savage.

****

Furcas and his son would be gone for nearly a week. This meant less work for Mama and me, two less mouths to cook for. This was not a rare event. The master often went on business trips around the county, around the state, and sometimes to other southern states. Since he'd taken his son, Jason, we knew where they'd gone. It was the annual trip to Colleyville to buy more slaves.

Every year, slaves would die, some from old age, some from overwork, some from brutal punishments at the hands of the plantation overseers or even Furcas, himself. These slaves needed to be replenished. The monthly slave auctions at Colleyville, well-known to all for their quality at low prices. Furcas would take his son on these excursions as part of his education. One day the Gethen Plantation would be all his, it was Furcas' job to make sure Jason would be ready when his time came. As well, they traveled with four overseers and two long wagons for the transport of the slaves he would buy with more than enough chains and locks to unsure no losses. Slaves can be expensive.

The mistress of the house and her daughter were easy to please. They ate very little and mother knew what foods they liked. All the food for the white overseers and the house slaves was cooked in a shack on the other end of the property. Having to cook for just half of the Gethen family was as close to a vacation my mother and I could ever expect.

A week later, I heard the sound of wagon wheels and chains. It was the master and his son returning from their journey. From the kitchen, we heard the familiar sounds of new slaves arriving. Only there was a strange sound other than the usual. There was the typical moaning; clanking of chains, only there was unusual shouting by the overseers and growling like the sound of a captured wild animal.

For dinner, we decided to prepare all the master's favorites. During preparation, young Thomas, one of the young lads who worked in the stables came with an armful of wood for the stove. As he stoked the fire, I asked about the gossip of the day.

"What was all the shouting about today?" I asked him.

Thomas was a year older than me, a wiry black lad with ears that stood out at the sides of his head like open shutters, a gap between his teeth so wide each word whistled out of his mouth. He shook his head at the question. "He scares me," he said, the word *scares* shrilled through his front teeth.

"What are ya sayin'? Who scares ya?" my mother asked Thomas.

Thomas continued to shake his head. "The new slave the Massa bought. He bought a dozen others, except this one is different. They needed to chain him from head to toe. They put him in a wagon all by himself, so he couldn't hurt the others."

He peaked both our interests. Mama and I gave him a look that pleaded with him to continue.

"I mean he's black like you or me, only he ain't like you or me. He's big, really big, as big as house, nearly two heads above everyone else. He looks wild. His hair all standin' up like so." Thomas held his hands a foot over his head to make his point. "He don't talk none, he just growls and howls. He bits and kicks at anybody who comes near him. They didn't only chain him they tied him, too. Took four overseers to get him into the barn, they got him chained and tied to one of the posts. When I looked at him, he just stared at me like a mountain lion. I had to look away. He's got the evil eye, I tell ya. I ran outta the barn before he took hold of my soul, or somethin'. He's evil, I tell ya, pure evil, got a demon inside of him, if he ain't one, he self."

Mama laughed, however, the look on Thomas' face stopped her cold.

After we cleaned the kitchen, we put everything in place to get a head start on breakfast in the morning, Mama and I left for home. It wasn't very late, still, it was dark. We couldn't help but pass by the barn. That's when we heard him.

The savage let out a holler like a banshee on its way to hell. We didn't know if we should run or turn back, we were so frightened.

Just then, two overseers came running to the barn. One of them held a few rags in one hand.

"The boss wants us to gag him so he don't yell all night long," the one holding the rags told the other.

They opened the barn door, standing there for a moment, afraid to enter.

"Ya ready?" one asked the other, as if they were preparing to ride a wild bronco.

"Be careful," said the other, "He's got a good head of teeth on him, and he bites."

They entered. We could hear the ruckus from outside.

We couldn't wait to get home to tell Papa and the others what we'd learned. Deidra and Lucius shivered as Mama told them all about it, just like when they'd heard a ghost story. Only, this was no ghost story, this was real. There was a monster among us, a real live monster.

I knew it was just my imagination. There was no way the beast could howl with a gag in his mouth. But, I could swear I heard him screeching in the night. I didn't sleep well, and when I did, I tossed and turned.

Two

New Blood

Colleyville was the largest city in the county with more two and three story buildings than any other city in the state, save for the capital. It was considered heavily populated without counting the folks who lived on the farms in the surrounding area. There were three hotels, three restaurants, five saloons, two public stables, not mentioning the dozens of businesses. Even the sheriff's office was a two-story with six cells on the second floor.

There was a railroad depot with a waiting room. Freight and passenger trains ran four to five times a day going north and south.

Known as a city of commerce, what made it famous was its slave auction every first Saturday of each month, excluding the winter months when weather conditions made travel hard to impossible.

The slave auction was a large event. Buyers and sellers of slaves would gather from miles around. All sales were conducted by the *Orson and Stanley Auction Company* for a small fee, of which a portion went to the city of Colleyville.

They erected a large stage at the end of Main Street near one of the public stables designated to house the slaves up for auction.

There was a carnival atmosphere during auction day. Storekeepers set up booths outside their shops to sell their goods. There was food and drink for sale, from pickled eggs to barbecue, from lemonade to whiskey.

Furcas and his entourage arrived the night before the auction, with intent to make an early day of it. Furcas got a suite at the finest hotel. His men would bed down at one of the flophouses on the outskirts of town. Normally on these trips, Furcas and his son would make an early night of it, dinner at one of the better restaurants, then back to the room for bed. Except this night would be different, Furcas had other plans.

After dinner, Furcas took the boy to one of the largest saloons in the city. The hoopla captivated the lad, the music, the gambling, the women, it all made his head spin. What made matters worse was Furcas gave the boy his first drink. If you've never drank a whiskey in your life, your first impression would be why would anyone drink such a brew, it's bitter, harsh, and it burns going down. Jason swallowed it down quickly, his eyes tearing up from the potency. He did his best not to show his distain for the concoction, fearing his father's disapproval of him, or worse, to laugh at him. To prove his manhood, he ordered another, drinking it down as quickly as the first, then another and another. To his surprise, the drink became smoother, less harsh till finally he was actually enjoying the taste and sensation. The liquid flowed through his veins till it got to his brain where it exploded like a Fourth of July celebration. Everything seemed funny. He laughed, his father laughed. One of the few times in his life the two of them ever laughed together.

The next stop that night was the *Crystal Palace* the ultimate gentlemen's club, which is a polite way of saying...*cathouse.*

The madam promised Furcas the lad would be in good hands. Everyone at the Crystal Palace knew it was Jason's first time; they could see it in his eyes and smile. The older men smiled that knowing smile they give to inexperienced younger men. The women flirted with him, wanting to be the one he'd pick to take him to the new world.

"He seems to like Dora," the madam whispered to Furcas.

"Any one but her," Furcas demanded. "She looks too much like his mother."

Furcas and the madam laughed.

The hours passed unnoticed, till finally Jason passed out in a drunken stupor. He woke up the next morning in his bed at the hotel. How he got there, he had no idea. Everything was fuzzy, especially his memory of what had happened.

****

Furcas made sure his overseers brought two empty crates for his son and him to sit on during the auction. It would be a long day, too long to remain standing.

On the stage a little, fat, white man with a loud voice was the auctioneer. They began bringing slaves from the barn onto the stage. The bidding started. There were men, women, old and young, children, couples, sometimes entire families. Furcas pointed out the pros and cons of each slave to Jason, what to look for. He had his own system for estimating the cost of a slave and how to bid. Jason listened carefully to every word his father told him. Eventually, Furcas allowed Jason to do some bidding.

"Not bad for your first time," Furcas said with pride. Jason bathed in the light of his father's praise.

At noon, the auction paused for an hour for everyone to have lunch. Furcas and Jason sampled the local barbecue. When offered a whiskey, Jason began to swim with the memory of the night before. Furcas just laughed, as Jason stuck to lemonade.

After lunch, the mood of the auction changed. Now was the time to auction off what they called *New Blood* slaves. This meant slaves that had just arrived from Africa. Many of them were living with their tribe in a village only a few weeks earlier. There was a different look about these slaves. The women and the children looked confused and frightened. The men looked defiant. It was clear they weren't sure what was happening or what was being said.

The bidding was low and slow. Not many slaveowners wanted to buy a slave without knowing their temperament.

"You know the mustangs that cross our land every few months?" Furcas asked Jason. The boy just nodded. "There was a time when we used to capture them and try to break them. It took much time and effort, and all we ever did was tame one out of a dozen. In the long run, I realized it was costly and not worth the time or money. I gave up the notion. That's what these slaves are like. Fresh off the boat, you don't know what their thinking or going to do. I think it's best to let someone else break them. When they've proven their worth, then I'll buy them."

Jason nodded his head agreeing, as if he'd heard the most important advice ever given. He'd heard the gospel of Furcas Gethen, understood it, taking it to heart – deep in his heart.

Just then, they brought onstage the most amazing looking black man, a slave for sale, a New Blood, straight off the boat from Africa. The crowd gasped as they guided him center stage. He wasn't large; the word didn't describe him well. He was monstrous, the size of a building. Not only was he chained, they tied him up with thick rope. There was a gag across his mouth. They found out later the gag was for protection. He spat at anyone within spitting reach, biting anyone who came within three feet. His clothes were torn. His hair stood on end. His eyes were afire like two hot coals of anger. His chest was the size of a washtub. His large muscles pressed against his worn clothing. It was clear he was big enough and strong enough to do the work of three men. Worth every penny to the man who could tame him, if that were possible.

To everyone's surprise, Furcas shouted out a bid, "Eight hundred!" All heads turned to see who this fool was. Jason looked up at his father, dumbfounded, his mouth open with surprise and confusion. This went against everything his father taught him.

"Eight hundred dollars," the auctioneer echoed, sounding as surprised as everyone else, bar that, he sounded relieved. The auctioneer knew as well as everyone else there would be no other bids, especially over eight hundred. Still, it was his job, and he was going to do it to the fullest, come hell or high water. "The bid stands at eight hundred dollars, can I get nine hundred?" No sound came from the crowd; no hand went up, not an eye flicker. "Can I get eight-fifty?" Nothing came again from the crowd. "Eight twenty-five?" Still, there was silence. "Eight hundred going once…going twice….sold to the gentleman and the young lad for eight hundred dollars!"

The crowd broke into cheers and applause, other than that, just as loud, if not louder, were laughs of disbelief and ridicule.

After the auction, Furcas decided they would leave for home, as he wanted to arrive back the next day. While, the overseers secured Furcas' purchases in the back of the wagons, he and Jason collected their things at the hotel, then went for a final meal at one of the restaurants before they left town.

Jason bent low, stretching across the table to whisper to his father. "Father, I don't understand. Each of your purchases today, you told me why you did it. Everything made sense to me. Except that last purchase, the big one, I don't understand. It went against everything you warned me about." Jason looked to his father with questioning eyes.

Furcas leaned back in his chair, sipped his whiskey, smiling at his son. "This man is possibly the strongest slave I've ever come across. He could easily do the work of three men."

"Yes, that's true," Jason replied. "That would be if he could be tamed. You, yourself, even said it would most likely be impossible to get him under control. And if you could, it would be too costly and time-consuming."

"You've learned well," Furcas said with pride. "That's true. That's why I'm not going to even try to tame him. I'll just keep him chained up all by himself."

Jason was completely confused.

Furcas laughed, "I'm not going to tame this animal; I'm going to tame his children."

Now, Jason was totally bewildered.

"You can't teach an old dog new tricks, but you can teach his puppies. This monster of a man will give his great physical attributes to his children. A bee such as he can pollinate many fields of flowers. Imagine ten, twenty, maybe thirty male children heirs to their father's strength, only raised by me to obey me and only me." Furcas was still smiling, very pleased with himself.

Jason sat back, looking at his father as if for the first time. He was amazed at his genius. "So, you're going to use this beast to spawn an entirely new species of slaves?"

"That's an interesting way of putting it. I never thought of it that way. Yes, that's exactly what I plan to do." Furcas finished his drink, waving to their waiter. "Our bill, please," he called out, and then turned to Jason. "We need to get going. I want to be back home sometime tomorrow."

****

Even bound he was dangerous, tossing his body about, slamming into the others. They chained the savage as well as tied him with a rope and then placed him in the back of one of the wagons, alone, by himself. He wouldn't let anyone near him. It was quite a feat for the overseers just to get him onto the back of the wagon. A few miles from town, he stopped tossing about, realizing he was no match for his bonds. Still, you could see the anger in his eyes, that he was just biding his time. The first chance he gets hold of someone would be their last.

The other slaves that Furcas bought sat quietly in the other wagon. Their heads bowed, they stared at the floor of the wagon. They'd been slaves all their lives. This was nothing new to them. All the fight in them, if it ever really was there, was gone. They looked at their brother from another world and time. *He'll learn*, they all thought to themselves.

Late into the night, Furcas halted the caravan. "We can rest here," he announced.

"We gonna spend the night here, Mr. Gethen? I can get the boys lookin' for wood. We'll have a fire goin' in no time," said Hackett, the head overseer.

"It's just a rest stop, Mr. Hackett," Furcas said as he dismounted his horse. "One hour, only. See that everyone is fed." He walked over to sit at the foot of a tree. He motioned for Jason to sit next to him. The father and son shared a canteen of water and some hardtack, as they watched the overseers feeding the slaves the same meal. They untied the hands and feet of the slaves, so they could eat and stretch their legs.

"What do ya want us to do with this one?" asked Hackett, standing at the other wagon, pointing to the savage.

"Unchain him, but under no condition untie his hands. Let him stretch his legs, take out his gag and give him something to eat, only keep close to him," Furcas ordered.

They did as they were told. They offered the savage water and some hardtack. He swallowed what was offered him in a flash, hardly chewing.

Watching from afar, Jason made an observation. "I just realized something," he said to his father. "All the slaves in the wagon huddle together, they eat together, and they talk among themselves. They seem to be somehow related, if not just in their predicament. Only they don't seem concerned with the big one, and he doesn't seem concerned with them. I don't understand. They're slaves, he's a slave. They're colored, and he's colored, except, they don't seem to want to know one another."

"It's simple," Furcas said. He pointed to the group of slaves eating near the wagon. "They all have the same mind-set. They know they're colored. They know they're slaves. They are all in the same boat. So, they bond, instantaneously." Furcas pointed at the savage. "He, on the other hand, doesn't see things as whites and colored. He only knows that if you're from his tribe, you are a friend. If not, you are a foe, or at least a possible foe. As for being a slave, he hasn't any idea what it means. He understands being a captive, and captives must do their best to escape. He will never give into submission. As for a feeling of comradery with the other group, he has none. He sees them as being no different from him than us. He feels alone."

Just then, Hackett offered another piece of hardtack, the savage's knee came up, slamming him in the groin. When Hackett bend forward in pain, the savage's tied fists came up into his face. The blow sent Hackett flying. The savage ran off into the darkness.

Furcas jumped to his feet. "After him, get him but I don't want him hurt, you hear me?" Furcas shouted.

Hackett and the other overseers ran into the darkness. Furcas and Jason took their guns from their holsters, covering the other slaves.

The other slaves remained motionless, staring at the ground. They had no intentions of causing any trouble.

There were shouts coming from the darkness, all around.

"Don't hurt him!" Furcas shouted into the abyss.

There were a few more shouts from the darkness, then silence. A few moments later, the overseers came to the wagons, dragging the limp body of the unconscious savage. They tossed him onto the back of the wagon, and rechained him. Hackett came up to Furcas and Jason, holding his hand over his ear. Blood was trickling down his arm.

"Bastard bit my ear!" Hackett declared.

Furcas said nothing about the matter. He smiled as if pleased. As if at that moment he realized he had made the right decision to purchase the beast.

Three

Asante

The next morning, gossip was in the air. Who or what did they have chained in the barn? Like all gossip, it was a collection of pieces that once put together made a whole, though not necessarily a complete or truthful one.

The two women who served breakfast to the Gethen family kept their ears perked. The workers in the field listened in on the talk between the overseers. Everyone questioned the stable boys, who were in and out of where they kept the savage locked away, especially Thomas who had a firsthand account. As the day came to an end there was enough available information to fill a newspaper.

That evening over supper in our home, mother and I pieced the rumors together for my father and siblings. For what it was worth, the story went like this:

Rumor was he was a king of his tribe. He had twenty wives and had over fifty children, which was only half of what his father the once king had, but then again he was still a young man. Slave traders attacked his village. He was the last man to be captured. He fought hard for three days, killing a dozen slave traders. They kept him tied up, separate from the other slaves on the boat coming over the ocean to the Americas for the safety of all. Furcas Gethen bought him for five thousand dollars, with the intent of taming him so he would have a worker who could do as much work as three men. As well, to break such a man would prove to the world he, Furcas Gethen, was stronger than any slave. All would fear him.

Of course, as I said, that was the rumors circulating the plantation. As for the truth based only on what little truths known, *they* went something like this:

True, he was from Africa, however no one knew exactly what part or even what tribe. He spoke no English. He spoke a language no one understood; although it was clear that whatever he was saying he said in anger. He was twice as large as most men, with muscles that were not to be believed until seen. His skin was dark black. His hair, now, cropped short and neat. If looked at carefully, one would say he was a handsome man, although few took the time. They were too busy trying to avoid him. And that is all the facts as were known at that time of this stranger.

In the middle of our meal and our speculation, there was a knock at the door. This was an odd thing to happen so late in the evening. We stared at the door, another knock. Papa rose from his seat, answering it. The dim light from our fireplace shone out into the darkness only a few feet, young Thomas stepped into the light.

"Thomas?" Papa said sounding puzzled. "What do ya want at this late hour?"

Thomas shuffled his feet, staring at the ground. "Massa told me to come here and fetch Audean back to the main house," he said, finally looking up into Joseph's face.

"That's ridiculous," Papa shouted. "She's just a young girl."

Thomas chuckled, "Shoo, taint nothin' like that there. The Mistress of the house is with him. They want her to come quick to the kitchen."

"Mistress of the house or not, it's late and. . ." my father insisted.

I rushed to Papa's side, pressing his arm. "It's all right, Papa. I'm a big girl. I can take care of myself."

"I just don't like it," Papa persisted.

"I'll be just fine," I said, kissing his cheek. "Besides, Thomas will stay with me, won't ya, Thomas?"

"Sure, I will."

Papa looked crosswise at Thomas. "Some comfort that be."

Thomas shot a look of defiance at my father mixed with a cheeky smile, as he took me by the arm, leading me into the darkness.

We walked around the main house to the backdoor, entering the kitchen. The room was poorly lit save for the red glow of the fire in the stove, which they kept burning day and night, and a lit hurricane lamp on the table. The flame was low, giving just enough light to make your way around, though I could probably do it blindfolded.

Furcas Gethen stood near the table. The lowlight of the lamp shone up into his face, causing shadows that made him look like a ghost. Even when he smiled, it looked evil. He was alone, no Mistress of the house as Thomas had ensured me. This was not what I expected. It didn't feel right.

"You may leave, Thomas. I need to speak to Audean alone," Furcas said.

Without question, Thomas left through the backdoor. Again, this is not what I expected. I tried not to show it, only I felt frightened.

"Sit down," he ordered.

I slowly obeyed, looking up into his ghostly face, waiting.

He spoke softly, not as if we were friends, but in a, dare I say it, in a fatherly manner. "What are the slaves saying about the man in the barn?"

I knew what he was asking so I came right to the point and told him what I'd heard. "There are all sorts of stories floatin' around," I said. "The only one that everybody seems to agree on is ya got a monster from Africa locked up in the barn."

He threw back his head, laughing loudly. "That might just be so," he replied. Then he slowly calmed down. He sat down in the chair opposite me. He became serious in his tone, yet remained friendly. "Can you read?" he asked.

This was a foolish question. Everyone knew it was against the law to teach a black slave to read and write. Even if they could, they would not answer such a direct question honestly. It would be many years later that I would learn such skills.

"Of course you don't," he corrected himself. "There's a French author who wrote a book about a man that everyone called a monster. He lived in a bell tower of a large church where he rang the bells for a living. No one wanted anything to do with him and he wanted nothing to do them. No one could approach him. Till one day he met a young gypsy girl. Because of her beauty and gentleness, she was able to get near him.

"I know how gossip moves through the plantation. I'm sure you've heard of the man I have locked in the barn. He's like that man in the book. No one can approach him. I've had my overseers bring him food, but he won't eat. If he dies, I lose a lot of money. I don't want to do that. I believe that just like the gypsy girl in the book you might be the one person he'd trust. I want you to fix him something to eat and bring it to him."

I was speechless. Even though he spoke to me with gentle words, I knew this wasn't a heartfelt appeal. I was his slave. This was a demand disguised as a request.

"Now...?" I asked, once I regained myself.

"Yes, right this minute," he replied as he left the kitchen. Before he was out the door he called back to me over his shoulder. "And no knives or forks, only spoons, not that he'd know what to do with them. I expect to learn in the morning that you were successful." With that he was gone.

I rose, standing for quite awhile pondering my predicament. When I could think of no alternatives, for there were none, I began to prepare a meal. A breakfast would be the quickest and easiest meal to make. I knew the savage was a large man that hadn't eaten in days, which meant he'd be hungry, hungrier than most men. On any given morning, my father could start the day with coffee, two eggs, fried potatoes, and a slice of bread. I decided not to make coffee; it would take too long. I scrambled four eggs, chopped and fried two whole potatoes, and sliced and toasted two thick slices of bread.

I left out the backdoor, holding a mug of water in one hand and the plate of food in the other, on it was a spoon. I moved slow and cautious, not only because I didn't want to spill anything but, because I felt scared, truly terrified.

The barn door was unlocked and left ajar, which I though to be odd. Using my foot, I opened the door. It was dark inside. A single lantern in one corner gave off just enough light to cast long shadows and make out silhouettes. I heard the sound of chains rattling off in the opposite corner. It was too dark to see anything; still, I could hear him stir. It frightened me, even though I knew he was chained. I walked over to the lantern. Placing the plate and mug on the ground, I raised the flame. The light was just enough to make out everything in a dim haze. I looked over to the opposite corner. I saw the savage jump to his feet, his chains jangled with his every move. I picked up the food and water, walking toward him. I stopped at what I felt was a safe distance. He stood there staring at me. He was large and muscular. Even from a distance, I knew I only stood up to his chest.

"Do ya want to eat? Are ya hungry?" I asked, holding the food out so he could see it. He just stared in silence. "This is for y'all," I said as I took a step forward, still keeping my distance.

There was a questioning look on his face, mixed with sadness. "Kwa nini unanifanya hivi?" he said in a soft grief-stricken tone. Don't ask me how I remember what he said. It was the way he said it that burned the words into my memory. Years later, I cried when I learned what he said. *Why are you doing this to me?*

"Here, eat." I placed the food and water at his feet. "Eat...eat," I said, making hand motions as if I were putting morsels of food in my mouth. He looked down at the plate of food. I suppose he was starving, or Gethen was right about the gypsy girl, either one or both, he fell to his knees and began to eat. He grabbed the food, proceeding to shovel it into his mouth by the handful.

"No...no, not like that," I said, hunkering down onto my heels. "Like this," I said, taking up the spoon, I gestured, bringing the spoon to the plate and then up to my mouth. "See! Yum...like that."

He took the spoon from me, examining it carefully. After a moment, he considered it useless. He let out a large laugh. His voice was deep and thunderous. I could feel it vibrate in my chest. "Haina Maana," he bellowed. Still laughing, he tossed the spoon aside, and continued eating with his hands.

"I guess it don't matter, no how, anyways," I said, watching him eat. "Ya smell like an old hog," I said, sniffing at him. "Well, I guess it ain't your fault, being chained up and all, day and night. I'll bring ya some soap and water, tomorrow."

He paid no attention to me. It didn't take him long to finish his meal. I found the spoon a few feet away, took up the plate and mug, slowly backing away from him. He stood up, again staring at me, only this time there was a hint of smile at the edges of his lips.

"I'll keep the lantern burnin' so ya can see. Ain't right to let ya live in the dark, like that. I guess I'll see ya in the mornin'," I said, slowly backing away, not wanting to turn my back to him. When I got to the barn door, I was just about to leave when he spoke.

"Asante," he said softly, a full smile on his face.

Instinctively, I knew what he said. He was thanking me.

"You're welcome," I replied, smiling back at him. "See ya in the mornin'." I turned and left, leaving the barn door ajar.

Four

Trust to Friendship to...

"What is he like?" my mother asked as she prepared breakfast in the kitchen of the main house for the Gethen family. "The savage in the barn, I mean."

"Just a man," I replied.

My mother sighed slightly, as if my answer disappointed her.

"What are ya doin'?" she asked me, noticing my tinkering about the kitchen. I'd filled a bucket with water that I warmed with some hot water from the kettle. I also had a bar of soap in one hand and a clean towel slung over my shoulder.

"I'm goin' to get him washed. He smells like an outhouse," I replied. I realized I used the term *he* when referring to the man in the barn. I could no longer bring myself to call him the savage.

The bucket was heavy; I sloshed most of it to the ground, as I made my way to the barn. I opened the barn door with my foot, leaving it wide open to let in the morning light.

"Good mornin'," I announced.

"Habari za asubuhi," he answered back.

He jumped to his feet when I entered. Much braver than I was the night before, I walked up to him, placing the bucket at his feet. I held the towel and soap to him. He just stared at it.

"Take 'em, take 'em," I said, pushing the items at him.

He caught on to my drift, taking hold of them. He held them in his hands, staring at them.

"Wash...wash," I laughed, lifting my arm in the air, mimicking a scrubbing motion.

He smiled, shaking his head, as he understood. He placed the towel over his shoulder, bent low dipping the soap into the water bucket. Lathering, he began to clean his hands and arms.

"That's right...that's right," I nodded, smiling. Again, I mimicked scrubbing my side and under my arms. "Wash...wash," I said.

I became a bit uncomfortable when he opened the front of his shirt and began to lather his chest. Because of his chains he was unable to take off his shirt. They rattled as he washed.

I couldn't help it. My gaze transfixed on his massive, muscular chest, as the soapy water made his wet chest hairs reflect like diamonds.

"That's it, ya got the idea," I praised him.

The next instant, before I could do or say anything, he undid his pant, dropping them to his knees.

"No...no, wait!" I shouted, turning my gaze from him.

I heard his deep, excessively large laugh behind me as I rushed to the barn door. I don't know what came over me. Before leaving, I looked over my shoulder to take one quick look. He was lathered from chest to his knees, and he was beautiful.

****

"Massa Gethen, can I ask ya somethin'?" I said, poking my head through the doorway of the main house library where Furcas Gethen sat alone, reading.

He shot a surprised look at me. We both knew I'd stepped over the boundary that separated master from slave. Many a slave received punishment for less. However, to my surprise he put his book down and smiled.

"Come in, Audean. Your mother told me that everything went fine between you and the savage. I heard you got him to eat."

"Yes, I'm going to bring him something in a few minutes. I also brought him water and soap to wash up. He was so filthy. Now, his clothes are still dirty. Would it be possible to get him some clean clothes?" I knew I was stepping my bounds, still I felt I had to try.

Again, he shocked me with a smile, agreeing to my request. "I can't see why not. I'll tell you what. I'll have the overseers remove all his chains, except for the collar around his neck that is chained to the post. We shouldn't be in such a hurry to relax our caution. Maybe in time, only I wouldn't advise it, yet. That way he can put on clean clothes. I'll have the overseers do it immediately."

It was not only astounding how civil he spoke to me, but how he took my advice, and how he confided in me. Still, I felt he was holding something back.

"Thank ya, sir, thank ya," I said, curtsying, and then turning to leave.

Before I was out the library door, he called to me. "It would seem you two have become friends."

"I wouldn't say that, sir, not friends. But, I would say he trusts me."

"Well, that's where it all starts, with trust, don't it?" he said laughing. "Often trust leads to friendship, and who knows where friendship may go?"

I shot him a side-glance of mistrust. I didn't feel comfortable the way the questioning was going.

He continued down a strange rabbit trail. "So, tell me, Audean, I'm curious. I've been around coloreds all my life and I still don't know what goes on in you folks' heads.

You're a young and pretty black girl. You should be coming into age, soon. Tell me, do you find this stranger attractive?"

I was utterly confused, now.

"I never thought about it," was my answer.

"Well, who knows what the future holds?" he laughed. "You may go, now," he dismissed me, going back to his book.

Walking back to the kitchen, an uncomfortable feeling washed over me. Something was going on in Massa Furcas' brain that I dare not think about.

'Do you find him attractive?' Of course I did; except, I wasn't going to admit it to him or anybody else, for that matter.

****

When I entered the barn with his meal, it relieved me to find him clean and dressed in new clothes. As Gethen promised, all his chains were gone save for the one attached to a post, the other end to a collar around his neck.

He stood up, pleased to see me. He gave me a smile, as large a smile as anyone might be able to muster under such circumstances. But there was a look in his eyes, dare I think it, a look of warmth.

I placed his meal at his feet. He got down on the ground, cross-legged, the plate and mug before him. Then something I never would suspect happened. He held his hands, palms down, over his food, bowed his head and began to sing. It was a strange and lovely song. I knew he was saying grace. Then he sat up, digging into his meal with both hands.

"Umm...umm," he said, nodding his head, smiling at me.

No longer afraid, I sat down on the ground in front of him. "I'm glad ya like it," I said. Then he again did something I least expected. He moved the plate toward me. Chained and hungry as he was, he offered me some of his meal. "No, thank ya, I already ate." He nodded, returning to his eating.

"Asante," he said, smiling when he finished eating.

I recognized the word from the last time he said it. "You're welcome," I said. His smile grew wider. It would seem he remembered my response to his *Asante*.

I was just about to take the empty plate when a thought struck me. "What is your name?" I asked. Of course, all he could do was look at me in bewilderment. "My name is Audean," I said. What a foolish statement to make to someone who didn't understand a single word. I decided the best approach would be the simplest. "Audean...Audean," I said slowly and clearly as I pointed to my chest.

When he understood, his head bobbed up and down. He pointed to me and spoke, "Audean."

"Yes…yes," I said as we both burst into laughter. I pointed to him, "What is your name?"

"Kujenga," he said softly.

"Kujenga," I repeated after him, hoping I pronounced it correctly.

"Ndiyo," he said, sounding very pleased.

He pointed to me, again. "Audean," he whispered.

"Ndiyo," I answered. This pleased him very much. I pointed to him. "Kujenga…"

"Yes…yes," he replied.

We both fell over, laughing.

****

In the slave quarters, it was all they talked about, Audean and the savage. Folks would stop me and ask me questions. "He's not savage," I insisted. "His name is Kujenga, and he's no different from us."

They'd look at me with astonishment; shake their heads as if I'd lost my mind, arguing against everything I told them about him.

"He may look like one of us, only he ain't," they'd say, "He's a savage."

Then there were myths, legends, and hearsay, "Those tribes in Africa live like animals. They kill their young. They eat babies. They kill their enemies and shrink their heads. They believe in human sacrifice and cannibalism."

I didn't know what to say to these people, not that they would listen. Even if what they believed was true, it wasn't true of Kujenga, I just knew it. Nevertheless, they didn't want to hear it. They didn't even want to know his name. He was the savage, that was all they knew, and all they cared to know.

My family was no exception; they too formed their opinion of Kujenga on rumors, gossip, and just knowing he was different.

"I hear he sharpened his teeth to fine points, like a mountain lion," my brother Lucius said, one night as the family ate dinner.

"Where did ya hear that?" I asked.

"All my friends say so."

"Well, your friends are all wrong," I snapped.

"Ya shouldn't look him straight on, they say he got the evil eye," my sister Deidra warned.

"Don't talk with ya mouth full," Mama reminded her. "Ya know Deidra's right. Some of those tribes from the old country got black magic."

I was just about to rebuke them when my father spoke. "I don't' care if he's a mountain lion or the devil himself; I don't like my daughter being near him."

I was just about to disagree. Then in a flash of wisdom beyond my years, I took a different approach, "But I got to do what Massa tells me to do."

Papa mulled this over for a moment. "Maybe so, but that don't mean ya gotta put your life in danger. Your job is to see that he's fed, and that's all I wants ya to do. From now on, I want ya to keep your distance from him. Don't get near him. Don't be friendly with him. Don't try to talk with him. Just keep aways from him, drop off his food and leave."

"And don't look him in the eye," my mother added, "Those people got the evil eye. They can put a curse on ya or steal ya soul."

☼☼☼☼☼☼☼☼

I never told anyone, lest of all my family, I continued to my visits with Kujenga, twice each day. I was never one to disobey my parents, but they were wrong. There was something good in Kujenga that was being buried by the cruel treatment he received, not only by the overseers but the other slaves, as well.

Days after my father's warning, I entered the barn with Kujenga's evening meal. I found him lying facedown on the ground near the wooden beam they nailed his chains into. I figured he was sleeping. Not wanting to startle him, I walked over as softly as I could.

"Kujenga," I whispered, hoping to gently wake him.

When I stood over him, I saw clearly what had happened. The back of his shirt was shredded, his blood poured out of him onto the floor. It was plain to see they'd whipped him into unconsciousness.

Kujenga…!" I shouted, dropping the plate of food. The clang of it stirred him. He raised his head slightly, looking at me. His lower lip was cut and bloody. His right eye was bloodred. This was not the result of being punched; it had to have been a kick from a heavy, hard boot. I fell to my knees, taking him up in my arms. His sad eyes looked up at me.

Why had they done this to him? The reason was simple and clear. They needed to break him. To have the upper hand, letting him know who rules him. Finally, submitting to being a slave.

Yet, I knew he would never give into them. He would sooner die. As well, I couldn't understand why they would do this. All this trouble and expense for one slave made little sense to me. Sure, as a worker he would be a great one. Except, it didn't seem worth it, they must have another reason, but what?

I held him closer. I didn't want him to see me crying. I wanted to run away, taking him with me. At that moment, I swore I would.

I looked once more into his eyes.

"Audean," he whispered.

Like a woman possessed, I leaned down slowly, pressing my lips to his. Our kiss was warm and deep. His lips were soft, tasting of salty blood. Despite our differences and the language barrier, at that moment, we were one.

Five

Africa's a Big Place

It was the smallest, most rundown shack on the edge of the slave's quarters. He lived alone, seeming to like it that way. He would speak politely when spoken to, although his answers were short, not leading to more talk. He never hurt a soul, be it in word or deed. Still, he moved about folks and the entire world as if he had no use for either one.

He was a wiry old man, boney. He swam within his clothes, his eyes always shaded by a floppy wide brim hat. No one knew how old he was. Some said he was the oldest person in the county, and I believed it. Though his skin was still smooth, there was something in his eyes that told you he was ancient.

They called him *Gloomy*. There seemed to be no known particular reason for calling him this. If there was an explanation, it was buried in the slave's graveyard, for the folks he'd lived his life around were long gone.

What drew me to him, to seek him out, was that of all the slaves on the plantation he was last of those who came directly from Africa. All the rest of us were born in the South, either on the Gethen Plantation or another and then sold to the Gethens.

I was nervous as I stepped onto his front porch. There was no need to knock on the door, the dried out old floorboards squealed under my step. The door opened; he stood in the doorway. I'd never seen him without his hat on. He was completely bald, smooth and shiny.

"Can I hep ya?' he asked, sounding friendly enough, though not necessarily enthused to having someone invading his world.

"Gloomy, I need to talk to ya."

"You be Joseph and Mary's oldest girl, ain't ya?"

"Yes, I am."

"Well, what'cha needs to talk about?"

"I wanted to ask ya about the past."

"What's to ask? Ya here today, ya were here yesterday and the day before. It be all the same. One day is as good as the other."

"I mean the long ago past. I want to ask ya about Africa."

His mood and expression changed. He looked at me solemnly, as if I'd asked about the passing of his mother.

"Come in, girl," he said as he turned, going back inside. I followed him. "Close the door, girl."

It was a one-room shack, made of the same squeaky gray wood as the porch. A small table and two chairs was in the center of the room, a small burning stove behind that, a one-person cot was against the wall under the only window, which was too dirty to look out of.

"Sit down, girl," he said, pointing to one of the chairs. "All I got is water and whiskey, and I ain't about to offer ya whiskey. Would ya like some water?"

"No, that's all right," I said, sitting down.

He pulled the other chair out from under the table, sitting down. "So, what's all this talk about the past and Africa?"

"Folks say ya came straight from Africa to here. It just sounds fascinating. I'd like to hear anything ya can tell me about it."

He gave me a side-glance. He wasn't buying it. "Hogwash," he chuckled.

I saw no reason to continue playing games. I'd lay all my cards down. "I'm the one who brings the food to the one they got chained up in the barn. I gotten to know him some and we've gotten friendly. But, he don't talk like we does, so he don't say much. I just figured ya might be able to help me understand him, where he came from and all."

Gloomy chuckled again, shaking his head, smiling. He called me out, "And ya like this boy, don't cha?"

"Yes, I do."

"In fact, ya love him."

It was as if he could read my mind. I looked at him in amazement. I felt no need to hide it. "Yes, I do love him."

Now, I can see some of you folks shaking your heads. Love…? You hardly know this boy, yet you say you love him. Jumping into the deep water a bit quick, aren't you? To these folks I ask to think back to when you were young…remember? Young love only needs a spark to turn into a bonfire. Yet, I do agree that with age those flames become bright coals, putting out warmth at a constant pace, forever. With age comes wisdom.

"Yes, I do love him. But how did ya know?"

"When ya been around as long as me, ya seen it so many times, ya know the signs. Besides, no one goes through all this trouble for a friend. If they're ya friend, they're ya friend, and that's it. But when ya in love, ya want more, ya want to know everything."

I began to see this old man in a new light.

Noticing my look of defeat, he encouraged me. "Don't fret. I'm gonna tell ya everything I know about Africa. But it ain't much. It was a long time ago." He stood up, walking to the stove. "If ya don't mind, if I'm gonna do this, I need a drink. And I don't mean water." He took a half-full bottle of whiskey and a filthy, cracked mug from off the one shelf on the wall. He placed them on the table, proceeding to pour a long drink.

"Let me think about this," he said as he sipped his whiskey. "It was so long ago. I was just a small boy at the time. I don't recall what part of Africa I came from, what country, what tribe; I don't even know what coast. Even if I did, it may not tell ya a thing about where yer friend came from. Africa's a big place, ya know?

"I do remember when it happened, the day they came for us, I mean. We lived in a small village, my parents and me. If I had any brothers or sisters, I don't remember. I don't remember the faces of my mother and father, only their shapes.

"We lived in huts and slept on the floor. I was in ours. My mother was cookin' somethin' over a fire in the center of the hut. That's when they came. There was shoutin' and screamin' all around. Some men from another tribe rushed into our hut. They hit my mother, hard. She fell to the ground. Then they dragged her outside. One of the men grabbed me, yankin' me by my arm. I was too young and too small to fight back. I tried with all my might, only it was useless.

"At first, I thought it was an attack from another tribe. There were strange black men runnin' after folks, hittin' them with clubs and then tyin' 'em up. But then I saw 'em, white men standing at the edge of the village, watchin' everythin'. I'd never seen a white man before. Heck, I never even heard of such a thing. They looked like people, only strange lookin', just the same. They covered themselves from their necks all the way down to their feet. I wondered how they could live all covered up like that.

"Once they rounded us all up, they tied our hands behind us and linked us together on a long rope. We began our march through the jungle to the sea.

"That day, that very hour was the last time I saw my parents. I looked frantically up and down the line of folks, but I never saw 'em.

"When we came to the ocean, I was in awe. I'd never traveled to the coast. I'd heard the ocean was big, but I had no idea. It looked as big as the sky. We huddled together. There were groups from other tribes as well, hundreds of people. I looked but I couldn't find my parents. Just offshore were three large ships. I had been in a canoe on the river with my father, but this was nothin' like that. They were so large I had no idea how it was possible they floated.

"Again, it was the strange black men who did all the work, while the white men stood around watchin', now and then shouting orders. They broke us up into small groups, herding us into longboats, rowin' each boatload outta one of the three ships.

"On board, all the strange black men left. We stood center deck surrounded by mostly white sailors, though there were a few blacks scattered here and there. They broke us into two groups: women and chillins along with the elderly, young to middle-aged men made up the other group. They put me with the men. There were two lower levels of the ship. They were to place the men at the lowest level and the other above 'em. Before they did this, they did somethin' that burned so deep in my memory I will remember every minute of it clearly till my dyin' day.

"Before takin' us below, they examined the two groups, carefully. Anyone they thought too weak, too sickly, or too old, this included the lame and the cripples, they shot and tossed them into the ocean. One bullet to the head and hurled overboard just like so much garbage. Everyone was frantic, women screamed, babies cried, and the men shouted. One or two of the men leaped at their captures. Healthy or not, they too were shot and thrown overboard. This they did as a warnin' telling all of us there was no hope.

"Down in the belly of the ship, they chained us to the walls. We lay down side by side with little room between us. We lay on top of one another. Hours later, we could feel the ship take sail, rocking back and forth till we were all dizzy. The darkness in the lower level made everything worse. It was two days before my eyes adjusted and I could make out the shapes of those around me. It looked like a fish market with the fish piled up in a straight line. The air was thick and heavy, making it difficult to breath. We sweat heavily throughout the entire voyage. What food they gave was of poor quality and just enough to keep us alive. By the third day, I was noticeably losin' weight, as were the others. Everyday when the sailors brought the food, they'd look for the dead. They'd unchain the bodies and take 'em away. As horrible as this was, we were grateful for the room this gave us.

"Every other day, they separated us into small groups and brought us topside. There, a sailor played a squeezebox. They forced us to dance to the music. The purpose for this was not only for us to stretch out legs, get some exercise, sun and air, which felt wonderful, but to judge our fitness. They watched, pointin' out the ones who couldn't keep up. Those who become too sickly or weak they tossed overboard. There was no need to waste a bullet to the head on 'em. We were too far from land, that anyone set adrift would die in seconds if they couldn't swim and hours if they could. I can still hear 'em screamin' as they fell from the ship, the splash, and then silence, just the sound of the waves hittin' the side of the ship and that damn squeezebox.

"I have no idea how long we were at sea. It felt like an eternity. By the time we came into port, our numbers were down to little more than half. They threw so many into the sea, both dead and those nearly dead.

"I never learned what port we landed at, it was on the east coast of the country, is all I can figure. After leavin' the ship, they took us to a slave auction where we were sold to white owners from miles around. Some of us went to plantations or farms, others to factories or to rich households. I was sold to a plantation, where for the next ten years of my life I worked in the tobacco fields. Slowly, I learned to speak English and get by. I was sold to another plantation, then another. I finally came here thirty years ago. It's been hard. I've never married, and pretty much stayed alone. I like it that way. I guess when I die no one will shed a tear. I certainly won't.

"That, my dear, is all I remember about Africa."

I was speechless for a moment.

"Can ya speak African?" I finally asked.

He laughed, "Girl, there ain't no such language. Africa is made up of many different tribes, villages, and countries. Africa's a big place. What one folk does and says at one end might not be the same as folk on the other end."

"Do ya know any words?" I insisted.

"I remember a little, but that don't mean I can talk to ya friend."

"His name is Kujenga."

"Kujenga, ya say? I recognize that word; it mean *Building*. They probably named him that because he's as big as one."

"Then you'll talk with him?"

"Hold on, girl, I didn't say no such thing." When he saw the sadness in my face, how I was close to tears, he changed his mind. "All right, I'll give it a try," he finally said. I reached over, giving him a hug. "That's enough of that. I said I'd give it a try, only. I ain't promisin' nothin'. Ya just don't tell anyone, ya hear?"

"I won't," I said as I stood up. "Thank ya so much." Before opening the door, I turned, asking one more question. "Why do they call ya Gloomy?"

There was a hurt look on his face for a moment. "I was just a boy at the time. I cried when they captured me. I cried often on the boat journey. I cried when they took us off the ship, and I cried all the way to the slave auction. Looking at me, one of the sailors said to another, 'Gloomy little bastard, ain't he?', and the name just stuck."

I left him staring at his mug of whiskey.

Six

No Words Could Ever Say

Each day, my mother became more upset with me. "Ya taken too much time deliverin' food to that animal they got locked up in the barn."

"He ain't no animal."

"Well, whatever he is, ya don't need to spend so much time around him. Ya need to bring the plate, come back, wait an hour and then go get the plate. He's too dangerous. He's got the evil eye. He'd put a hex on ya. Ya hear me?"

"Yes'um."

However, I never obeyed. Eventually, she grew tired of hearing herself talk, I guess, because she stopped warning me. I was just glad she never told my father, or there would have been hell to pay.

I just couldn't help myself. I wanted to be with Kujenga, as often as possible, for as long a time as possible. I could tell he felt the same. Though we spoke different languages, we understood each other. It's all in the eyes, the smile, and the touch. I'd sit before him as he ate. Without saying a word, we were having the time of our lives. The first time he reached out, taking my hand, I knew for certain. I still get chills thinking about it.

****

It was evening; I came to fetch Kujenga's dinner plate. At first, he smiled when he saw me, and then his face went blank when he saw who was with me. He watched the old man's every move. He wasn't afraid, but then who could be afraid of Gloomy? Still, he stood up, wearing a look of uncertainty.

Gloomy walked up slowly to Kujenga, looking him in the eye. "Fadhili," Gloomy said softly, clearly trying to sound friendly.

A smile exploded on Kujenga's face; his eyes went wide, like a sailor lost at sea when he sees land off on the horizon. He began rattling off in his native language. He believed he'd found a brother, and he had so much to say. It flowed from him like a river.

"Whoa there, hold on! I only know a couple of words," Gloomy said, holding his palms to halt him.

Immediately, Kujenga understood. His smile left him. A look of sorrow and disappointment enveloped him like a black veil over the deceased. He realized that once again he was alone. He looked to me, his only friend.

"It's all right. Gloomy is here to help," I said, reaching out to him. He was about to take my hand when he turned to Gloomy.

"Mwambie ni kumpenda," Kujenga said, looking very solemn.

"What did he say?" I asked.

Gloomy looked at me. "He told me to tell you that he loves ya."

I took hold of Kujenga's hand; we looked into each other's eyes. "Tell him I love him, too."

The old man's eyes went from me to Kujenga then back to me. "I think he knows."

****

For an hour, Gloomy and Kujenga sat on the ground facing each other. They both searched their minds for words that both knew and understood. Eventually, they shook their heads, laughing, knowing there would be no conversation, today. Gloomy only understood enough of what Kujenga said to ask casual references, unrelated to what was at hand. As for Kujenga's English, he knew only three words: Yes, No, and my name.

Kujenga helped the old man to his feet.

"Well son, at least we tried," Gloomy said as he brushed the dirt off his pants.

The two smiled at each, finally hugging farewell.

"Good-bye," Gloomy said, heading for the barn door.

"Good-bye," Kujenga echoed to the old man.

Again, they both laughed.

"Thank ya," I told Gloomy.

He smiled back at me. "At least we tried," he repeated as he left.

I picked up the food plate from the ground.

"I have to go," I told him.

He reached out to me, pulling me close to him. Holding me in his strong arms, he reached down, kissing me. This kiss was different from any other kisses we shared before. There was still that sweetness, only now there was an undertone of passion, a fire that burned within us.

Pulling away from him, I smiled at him before leaving the barn.

"I love ya," I said.

He tried to mimic me. "I love ya," he said awkwardly.

Instinctively, we both knew what the other said.

****

Late that night as I lay in bed, I couldn't sleep with the image of Kujenga so clear in my mind. I could still feel the touch of our last kiss on my lips, the warmth now turned into a roaring flame.

As quietly as I could, I got out of bed, grabbed my clothes, and walked through the house, heading for the front door. The wood floorboards were like guard dogs barking up at me. I went as slow as possible to minimize the noise. It must have taken me a good fifteen minutes to get out of the house.

Once outside and off the porch, I changed into my everyday clothes, folding my nightgown, hiding it behind a shrub.

The night was dark; it was only a half-moon. I walked as silently as I could, making my way to the barn. Opening the barn door, I looked in. Someone left the lantern on a low flame in the far corner. I went to it, bringing the flame up just enough to see, still keeping it low. Long shadows danced across the floor and walls. The only sound was the gentle wind outside rustling the leaves in the trees.

I walked to Kujenga who was sleeping on the ground. He lay on his side, trying to keep warm. He looked so at peace. I got down on the ground, watching him sleep. He was the most beautiful sight I'd ever seen in my life. No sunrise or sunset could compare to him.

I reached out, gently stroking his cheek. His eyes burst open. He quickly sat up. His body stiffened, ready for anything. When he realized it was me, he went limp, smiling at me.

"Oh, Kujenga," I whispered, falling into his arms.

His arms flew around me, he held me close and hard. I'd never felt so safe in all my life. For whatever reason, I began to cry.

"Shh," he hissed, pushing his mouth against my ear.

His hands moved across my back, as he rocked me in his arms.

"Shh," he kept repeating, as if to say everything was going to be all right.

He backed his head away slightly. I looked up into his eyes. His head descended slowly till our lips met. Again, it was that special kiss, filled with a love no words could ever say.

Before we knew it, we were on our sides, kissing in a deep embrace. The sound of our breathing filled the barn, the echo coming back to us. This was all new to me, yet it felt so natural. His hands on my body, warm, exploring, trebling. I knew at that moment, he was no more experienced in the ways of love than I. We would learn together.

Our lips never parted. I moved my hands over his arms, feeling his strength, to his massive shoulders, then behind his neck pulling him down on me. I worked my hands under his shirt, running them over his chest, catching his manly hairs between my fingers.

With one hand, he fought with the buttons of my blouse, till it was open and he moved his hand inside.

"Take your hands off of her, ya savage!" the words shattered the night.

Like a shot, we sat up. Standing at the barn door was my father holding a thick wooden beam in one hand. He came rushing toward us. Before either one of us could react, my father wheeled the beam around, hitting Kujenga on the side of the head – hard. Kujenga went down. But that wasn't the end of it. My father continued to beat Kujenga with the beam. Hitting him between every word he shouted. "Never...touch...my...daughter...again."

Wrapping my arms around my father's legs, I cried out, "No, Papa, stop, you'll kill him!"

He broke free from my grasp, backing away, pointing the piece of wood at me. "Ya get home, girl, right this instant, ya hear?" he shouted.

"Don't kill him, Papa, please don't kill him," I cried.

"I will if ya don't get home, right now!"

Not having time to button my blouse, I held it closed, got to my feet, starting for the barn door. I was so relieved when I sensed my father walking behind me. Outside the barn, he tossed the piece of wood off into the distance. Still holding my blouse closed, we started for home.

To add insult to injury, my father took off his belt, proceeding to whip me across the back with it.

"I warned ya! I don't want ya ever to go to the barn, again. I don't ever want ya to see that beast, again!' he hollered between the whippings.

"He's not a beast, Papa. I love him!"

My father had no answer to this only to whip me harder.

When we got to our home, I stumbled falling onto our porch, my father never stopping his lashing. Dressed in her nightgown, my mother came out, rushing onto the porch, falling to her knees, taking me into her arms.

"Joseph, what are ya doin'? This here's our daughter."

"Do ya know what your precious daughter's been doin'? I caught her half naked in the arms of that savage."

"Is that true?" she asked me, looking into my eyes.

There was no need to answer; she understood the look on my face.

"I can't say I approve," my mother said. She looked to Papa, "But I recall, it ain't no different than when we two got together. We can talk this out. Beatin' her ain't gonna change her mind." She looked at me. "Go to bed, child."

I struggled to my feet, entering our home. I could hear my mother speaking softly. "Joseph, we need to talk."

Seven

That's His Name

Early the next morning as our family prepared for the day, there was a knock at the door. My father answered it. It was young Thomas. We'd grown to be apprehensive of Thomas' visits. More often than not, he had sad or upsetting news to tell.

"Kind of early, ain't ya, boy?" my father said, standing in the doorway.

"Massa says he wants to see ya right away, and bring your daughter, Audean, with ya."

"What's he want?" my father asked.

"He don't tell me the what for or the why for. He just tells me to tell Joseph to get here, now, and bring his daughter."

"Tell 'em I'll be right there," my father replied.

"No, Massa says right now. If he's eatin' or he's puttin' on his pants and only got one leg in, tell him to stop and come here," Thomas said, strongly.

Papa turned to me. "Come on, girl, let's get it over with."

We followed Thomas to the main house. Halfway there, Thomas bowed out, starting off in another direction.

"Where ya think your goin'?" my father asked.

"I don't want to get involved, no way, no how. I done did what I had to do, and I'm gone. Ya two are on your own. Good luck."

We didn't talk to each other, as we walked on. We went straight to the main house. On the porch, Papa knocked on the door.

To our surprise, Furcas Gethen, himself, answered the door.

"Ah, Joseph, good, follow me," he said, turned and walked down the hall. "Close the door behind you," he ordered without looking back.

Though he only spoke to my father, I understood I was to follow also. He took us to a large room with a high ceiling, the library, a grand room it was. Shelves filled with books covered all the walls save for the outer wall with four wide windows overlooking the barn. Off to the right of the room was a large desk, where all of us stood, next to the desk was a world globe on a pedestal. With one hand, Gethen constantly spun the globe as he spoke.

"This is a beautiful room, isn't it? Look around, Joseph, tell me what you see." Without waiting for a response from my father, Gethen went on. "Lots of beautiful and expensive things and it's the same in all the other room of this house. I can afford it; I'm a very rich man. All of this is mine."

Gethen stopped the globe with the flat of his hand. He walked over to the fireplace. There was a stack of cut firewood. He took a log off the top, walking back to us with it. He handed it to my father.

"Here you are, Joseph. Take another look around this beautiful room, at all the expensive finery that belongs to me. Now, tell me, which one of my things would you like to smash with that there piece of wood? That big vase over there, or perhaps you'd like to knock down all the bookshelves?"

"No, sir, I don't," my father mumbled, looking down in embracement.

"What's that?" Gethen shouted. "Speak up; I didn't hear you!"

"No, sir, I don't want to break up none of your things."

"Oh, you don't, do you?" Gethen said, taking the piece of wood from my father. "Then tell me why you tried to destroy one of my prized possessions? You think I don't know what goes on around here on this plantation? I know you put a beating on that boy we got locked up in the barn. That's my property. If I want to put a beating on him, then I'll do the beating, not you. Don't you ever so much as lay a finger on anything that belongs to me."

Without warning, Gethen rammed the piece of wood into my father's gut, buckling him over, sending him to the floor on his knees.

"Listen to me, Joseph," Gethen said, waving the piece of wood in father's face. "If you ever try to play the master in my house, again, I'll kill you. I swear I will. You understand me, Joseph?"

"Yes, sir, I do."

"Now, get up and get out of my sight."

Papa placed his hand on the edge of the desk to help get back onto his feet. Gethen brought the piece of wood down, smashing my father's fingers.

"I just told you not to lay a finger on any of my things. Now, get out of here."

In pain and with great difficulty, my father got to his feet, walking to the door. I started following my father when Gethen held the piece of wood in front of me as a barricade. "Not you, I want to talk to you."

I remained in place. My father turned and looked at me with sorrowful eyes. There was nothing either one of us could do. Using his unhurt hand, he opened the door and left the room, closing the door behind him.

Gethen placed the piece of wood back in its place near the fire. "Don't worry, I'm not going to hurt you," he said as he approached me. He leaned against the side of his desk, as he spoke.

"You've become quite friendly with that boy in the barn," he stated bluntly.

I didn't say a word.

"I'm not mad, if you did. You can tell me."

I whispered my answer. "Yes, sir, I have."

"In fact, you've become more than friends, haven't you?"

I didn't answer, but knew I showed the statement to be true by how embarrassed I looked. He laughed, pointing to the chair in front of the desk. "Sit down; I've got a proposition for you." I didn't move. "Go ahead; I'm not going to hurt you. You can sit down."

Hesitantly, I sat down, looking up at him.

He continued, "Do you know why I bought that big brute?"

I remained silent.

"Go ahead. You must have thought it strange that I would spend so much money just to keep him locked away. What do you think is the reason?"

I was slow and timid with my answer. "Because he's so big?"

"Well, that is a large part of it. But so what, so he's big. Why would that matter?"

"Because he can do more work than any man?"

"Again, you're right, only what good is it if he can do more work if I can't get him to work?" He laughed, again, when he realized I was stumped. "True, I bought him because he's big and he could be a good worker." He hesitated to make sure he had my full attention. "I bought him so he could father babies. They'll be babies that will grow as big and strong as he is, only I will raise them, and they won't disobey me."

I still wore a questioning look.

"He likes you. He trusts you. I want you to have a baby with him."

"Ya want me to marry him?"

Gethen let out a laugh that shook the room. He nearly fell to the floor. "No, did I say that? I said I want you to have his baby. Marriage is the last thing I want for him. He's like a bee, and a bee can pollinate many flowers. That's what I want him to do. I want to have as many women as he can handle. I want him to father as many babies as possible, preferably, more boys than girls."

I didn't know what to say or do. I felt confused and scared. Finally, I mustered enough courage to speak. "I won't," I said.

"How's that...?" Gethen asked, still laughing. "I'm afraid you don't have a choice. Like that big brute in the barn, you are my property; you will do as I say."

I stared down at the floor and began to cry. "Please...don't...I can't."

"But there *is* something between you two?" he said, his laughter started to fade.

"Please...not that way," I wept.

He stood up straight before me, looking down on me with a stern face. I looked up at him. He spoke coldly, matter-of-factly.

"Very well, you don't have to do it if you don't want to. But from now on you don't go near that barn. You will never see him again. You will only see the women he has loved and the children he has fathered." He stopped for a moment of thought, then smiling, as if something wonderful materialized in his brain. "From now on, I want all his meals brought to him by your father, not you, not your mother, only your father. That should teach him. Now, get out of here, go home, and tell your father my decision."

I rose from the chair, heading for the door. Just as I was leaving, he made one last remark.

"Oh, and if I ever catch you near that barn, if you so much as stick your head in through the door, I will have you whipped so severely your own mother won't be able to recognize you."

✶✶✶✶✶✶✶✶

Mother and I worked the rest of the day in the kitchen. We spoke not a word to each other. The air between us was thick, heavy, and uncomfortable. Kujenga would have no food that day, as I would not see my father till the evening to tell him he would be taking the food to the barn, from now on. I dreaded the thought of having to tell him.

When we got to the house, we found Deidra and Lucius sitting on the porch.

"What are ya two doin' sittin' out here?" Mama asked. She looked at Deidra. "Ya should be inside startin' supper."

"I was tryin' to, but Papa kicked us out," Deidra replied.

"He's mad as a rooster in the rain," Lucius added. He looked up into my eyes. "He said he wants to see Audean as soon she got home."

Mama and I walked onto the porch.

"Papa said he only wants to talk with Audean," Lucius cautioned Mama.

"He does, does he?" Mama said, ignoring the words of warning, as she opened the front door. I followed. Once inside, I closed the door.

Papa stood at the far end of the room, staring at us. There was a strange look about him. He swayed back and forth and from side to side. His eyes watered, as if he were about to cry.

"Joseph, you're drunk!" Mama declared.

"Damn right, I'm drunk," Papa said, staggering a few steps forward. He pointed at me. "I've always wanted the best for ya. I don't do these things because I hate ya; I do them because I love ya. Now, Massa puts me in my place. I ain't even got the right to be a father, he says. Hell, I ain't even got the right to be a man."

Mama walked to Papa, gently guiding him to sit at the table. "Sit down, Joseph; I'll make ya some coffee."

I sat down in the chair next to him, taking his hand in mine. "I love ya, Papa."

He smiled at me through tear filled eyes.

I didn't know if it was the right time, but I thought it best to get everything out in the open. "Papa, Massa says ya gotta be the one to bring Kujenga his meals."

"Who…?"

"Kujenga, Papa. The boy in the barn…that's his name."

Eight

Too Warm to Sleep"

As time passed, my heart became heavy. I missed Kujenga, deeply. My father received permission twice a day to leave his work in the fields to delivery Kujenga's meals. I wanted so much to ask my father how Kujenga was; only I was too afraid to ask him. He never said a word about it. It was heartbreaking for me.

In my sorrow, I realized Massa Gethen's plan. He understood how I felt about Kujenga. He was betting I would cave in, agreeing to have Kujenga's child. Only, I wanted more. I wanted to marry him.

Even if I did consent to Gethens' demands, I would only be the first and only one of many women he planned for Kujenga. That was another torture. If Gethen gave up trying to persuade me, he might bring one of the other slave girls into it. And if he did, would Kujenga accept the offer? I didn't sleep much during that time.

I felt so alone. There was no one I could think of confiding in, not my mother, my sister, or any of the other slave women. Strangely enough, the sympathetic ear was Gloomy. I visited the old man often over the next few weeks. I told him everything. He understood, offering good advice.

"There are only two paths ya can take," he told me. "Ya either give him up..."

"I'll never give him up," I broke in.

He ignored my outburst, continuing his guidance. "Ya can either give him up or do somethin' about it. That would be y'all runnin' away together."

"Where would we go?"

"If it was me, I'd go to Mexico. It's far off and it would be dangerous. But, once y'all are over the boarder, ain't no body goin' to go after ya. Besides, Mexicans don't care none about color."

My mind raced with ideas. I'd seen others who tried to escape. I never knew of anyone who succeeded. They were all caught, brought back, either hanged or whipped to death.

"Don't decide right away," Gloomy said. "Take your time; think about it. There are dangerous possibilities to each path. If ya try to run away and ya get caught, it will mean your life. Are ya willin' to die for this man?"

I nodded I would. "And what is the other dangerous possibility? If I give him up, what other evil could befall me?" I knew I never would give up my love, but I had to know his answer.

He looked so serious as he whispered. "Ya may never love again."

Like a hunger that continues with no relief. The thought of Kujenga was in my mind constantly. All-day long, working in the kitchen, the remembrance of him was with me. At night as I lie in bed with my eyes closed, the vision of him was always there. My skin burned with the memory of his touch. Sleep came with great difficulty and stayed for too short a time.

It was a warm night, too warm to sleep under the covers. On the other side of the room, Deidra and Lucius were in their beds fast asleep. The light of the half-moon poured in through the window, giving clarity to only shape and form, but not color. Everything was bathed in a blue-gray haze.

With no regard for consequences, I decided I would go to Kujenga. I realized what I'd done wrong the last night I visited him. How my father knew I'd gone to him, following me to the barn. That night I left out of the front door, the squeaky floorboards in the house and the porch gave me away. This night, I would sneak out the window only a few feet from my bed. Being such a stifling night, the window was already open. Not wanting to take the chance of waking anyone, I decided to leave my clothes draped over the chair at the foot of my bed, where I left them, my shoes under the bed. I'd go to Kujenga in my nightgown.

Sliding down the side of the house slowly, my nightgown ripped slightly along a nail. There was a thin line of blood where the nail cut me. I backed away from the house slowly trying to not rustle the leaves on the ground all around the house. Though it was a warm night, my bare feet felt chilled.

There was just enough light to make my way to the barn. Before opening the barn door, I looked to the main house, examining the windows fearing Gethen was watching. The main house was dark. All was quiet.

The barn door was slightly ajar. I wriggled my way in. The small flame burning in the lantern on the far end of the barn was just enough light to make my way to him. He slept on his side. I got down on the ground next to him, watching him sleep. There was a smile on his face as he mumbled. He was dreaming. What could he be dreaming about? Was he once again home in Africa, running with his friends through the jungle near his village? Then his face contorted; he began to mumble and moan. No longer was he dreaming of Africa. Reality set into his dreams. He was thousands of miles from his home, chained like an animal, sleeping on the ground. Even in his sleep there was no peace.

"It's all right," I whispered, reaching out to him.

His eyes burst open. A look of fear was on him till his vision cleared and he saw my face.

"Audean," he said, smiling. He reached out; his large hand cupped the back of my head. He gently pulled me closer till our lips met. I fell into his arms as we kissed. His lips were soft and warm.

Our lips parted. He guided me onto my back, smiling down on me. It was then he noticed the tear in my nightgown and cut on my thigh, which already began to heal. He bent low, kissing the wound. I thought of when I was a child, how my mother would kiss my hurts and make them better. Kujenga kissed my hurt, and the world became better.

He moved over me, his lips stopping every few inches, kissing, his large hands moved over me like a low flying clouds over hills and valleys. He moved up till we were face-to-face. He positioned himself squarely on top of me, his weight holding me down, like a heavy blanket. I never felt so secure and safe in my life. The thoughts of my inexperience in the ways of love disappeared. All that mattered was that we wanted to be with each other. Each wanting to make the other happy, and within that bond, we could do no wrong. All fear vanished.

So, this was love. Why had no one ever told me? Perhaps, their love was not like this, so they described it so poorly. Or maybe words cannot describe it, always coming up short, so no one ever tries.

I was sure no one since the beginning of time ever kissed as we kissed. No one ever loved as well as we loved.

****

I woke, looking out at the world through the slightly ajar barn door. There was a faint blue glow to everything. It would be dawn, soon.

"I have to go," I whispered, being held tightly in Kujenga's arms. I gently broke free, sitting up. "I have to go," I repeated. He nodded understandingly.

I kissed him once more; then standing up, I adjusted my nightgown. His eyes never left me as I backed away slowly toward the door. Not wanting to prolong the pain of separating, I turned and left.

The world was becoming clearer as the beams of sunlight shot up over the horizon. I ran home. It was far more difficult climbing into my window than it was crawling out of it. I got into bed; pulling the covers up to my chin, I closed my eyes.

Not more than five minutes passed when my mother entered the room.

"All right, sleepyheads, time to get up," she said loudly. "Come on, get up, breakfast is ready in five minutes."

Every morning it was the same ritual of a mother trying to stir her sleeping children. Deidra and Lucius groaned, turning in their beds, pulling the covers over their heads. Not wanting to act suspicious, I let out a sleepy moan.

Mama stood over my bed. "Come on, girl. We gotta get to the main house to cook breakfast," she announced, pulling the covers from off me.

Immediately, she knew something was wrong. She saw the tear in my nightgown and the cut on my thigh. Also, she noticed something I hadn't thought about. My feet were filthy from running barefoot.

At that moment, she understood. "Oh, child, what have ya done?" she whispered sorrowfully. She was aware this was not the time or the place for a discussion. So, she trudged on. "Wash ya feet, before ya father sees 'em," was all she said. Then she left the room, returning to the kitchen.

All through breakfast, I stared at my plate, embarrassed to look my father in the eye, ashamed to look to my mother. Though he didn't know it, I'd let my father down. My mother knew it. Still, thinking back, I didn't regret what I did.

Like every morning, my father was the first to leave. He kissed his wife good-bye, then his children. When his lips touched my cheek, I knew how much I loved and respected my father. I wanted never to hurt him. Still, I knew if I continued this path I was on, there would be no avoiding it.

Mother and I walked to the main house in silence. At the halfway point, Mama stopped and turned to me. "What are ya thinkin', child. Do ya want to break my heart and kill your father?"

"Ya know that's not true," I snapped. "I love ya both, but I love Kujenga."

Mama sighed, "That's right, that is his name, isn't it? Don't ya understand, Audean? He don't speak like us, he don't think like us, he don't act like us, he ain't one of us."

"We don't need words," I announced. "I trust the way he thinks. He acts with bravery and honor. He don't have to be one of us. He just has to be one with me, and he is."

Mama shook her head. "Ya sound just like a woman in love. I should have known it would happen someday. I just didn't think it would happen like this. I suppose ya can't help or stop who ya love," she wisely said. We continued walking. "Just don't tell your father," were her last words.

Nine

Not in Words, Maybe

We just finished preparing breakfast for the Gethen family, when the backdoor to the kitchen swung open. Two overseers entered. At the same moment, the door from the house into the kitchen opened. In walked Furcas Gethen, marching straight up to me. I looked to my mother. Her face was filled with fear. I could image mine looked the same.

"I warned you," he shouted into my face.

I was speechless.

"I told you nothing happens on this plantation that I don't know about."

I knew he was talking about my visit to Kujenga. Except, how did he know? Did he see from one of the windows of the main house, me going in or out of the barn? But all the lights were out. Did he sit by the window in the dark, waiting? Did he have one of the overseers watch the barn door, day and night? None of it sounded reasonable.

"Take her," Gethen ordered the overseers. "We need to make an example of her. Let every slave know my will is law."

With that, the two overseers took hold of me, pulling me out of the backdoor, around the building to the front of the house.

There was a large brass bell on the porch. An overseer took a hammer to it, ringing it loudly over and over. Its peal filled the air for miles. Everyone knew what it meant, to gather at the front of the main house to witness punishment to a slave, be it a whipping or a hanging. All slaves of the Gethen Plantation must witness the punishment, no exception.

All, including myself, felt relieved to see one of the overseers wheeling a whip of cowhide. It would be a nightmare of a punishment, but not the end of my life. Bodies survive whippings, the skin torn open till blood flows. But, no one survives the grave except in the Bible, other than that, definitely not on the Gethen Plantation.

I frantically looked around. My eyes caught a glimpse of my family. Deidra and Lucius looked bewildered. My mother was in tears, using her apron to dry her cheeks. My father was like a mainspring ready to snap with flames of anger blazing in his eyes. I felt more worried for him than myself.

Two of the larger overseers held me spread-eagle over the back of a wagon, pushing my face down. Everyone went quiet. The atmosphere was empty except for the sound of crows off in the distance. When suddenly the whoosh of the whip cutting through the air broke the silence like a thunderclap slashed through my blouse and into my flesh.

I screamed loud and long. I knew it would hurt; only the reality was far greater than I anticipated. Again, the whip came down, and then a third time. Each time I shouted in pain. I felt surprised and relieved when the overseers released me. Normally, three stripes across your back was just the beginning. Why was I spared? I could only assume Gethen wanted me punished only to a certain point to show me and the others who was Massa and who was slave. Possibly, he still held hopes I would agree to his terms about Kujenga. He didn't want me too badly damaged.

I backed away from the wagon. Along with the pain, I felt the sticky wetness of blood dripping down my back. I spun around. Trying to walk, I stumbled about like a drunk. The next thing I knew, my mother was at my side, guiding me away, guiding me home.

As we walked past the barn, a bloodcurdling screech came from inside. Kujenga heard my cry of pain. It was like the howl of wounded animal. The sound of it filled everyone with fear. But not me, I knew why he cried out. It was a cry of anger mixed with sorrow. He cried for me, and I for him.

||*|*|*|*|*

"What were ya thinkin'?" Papa shouted at me from the doorway of our bedroom. I lay facedown, as Mama cleaned the welts on my back from the whip.

"Ya puttin' all our lives in danger!" my father continued.

I didn't say a word. I knew he was right. Still, the heart wants what the heart wants. Though the Bible says if you listen to your heart you're a fool, for it will guide you down the wrong path. That might be true, but it does sing the sweetest song. I was so confused.

Papa's voice became calm, "Promise me ya won't ever try to see that boy, again."

I didn't want to hurt or disobey him, but it was a promise I never could keep.

"I can't, Papa," I cried into my pillow. "I love him."

"I don't believe this girl," he said. I couldn't see him but I knew he was pacing the floor, shaking his head.

"I only hope nothin' comes of all this," Mama added.

I could tell Papa stopped his pacing. "What do ya mean?"

"I mean, she spent the night with this boy."

"So…?"

"Figure it out, Joseph. She might be in the family way."

"It was only one night," Papa insisted as if speaking some unwritten law.

"Joseph, after three children ya should know better. It only takes one night, or don't ya remember?"

A long moment of silence passed before Papa spoke. "Ya don't think…?"

"I don't think nothin'," Mama answered. "She is or she ain't. We'll know soon enough."

"There's ways to stop such things, ain't there?" Papa asked, shyly.

"Yes, there is," Mama replied. "Only them things don't happen in my house. Now get outta here and close the door behind ya. I need to talk with my daughter."

When I was sure Papa left the room, I rolled over.

"Your father's right, "Mama said. "Ya causing a heap of trouble for ya'self. And ya ain't doin' that boy no favor, either."

My eyes began to well up.

Mama continued, "I ain't ever known a young girl that had a lick of sense in her head. They got no brains, just heart." She hesitated before going on. "Ya love this boy, don't ya?"

"I do, Mama."

She let out a long sigh. "If ya pregnant, ya gonna be the one to raise it. I done had three babies, thank ya. I've done my share."

"Mama, I gotta get word to him, somehow."

Mama shook her head. "Well, I don't know how ya can. Ya was lucky this time. They catch ya again; they'll whip ya to a cripple."

"Then ya tell him, Mama."

"I love ya, child, and I feel for ya. But, I ain't never gonna go behind my husband's back. He ain't always right, but he is my husband. When ya children are up and gone, he's all I'll have left."

****

Children should be seen but not heard. This does not take into account what the children hear. When a family lives in such a small shack, there are no secrets. Unknown to my parents or me, Deidra, sitting at the dinner table, heard every word. Lucius was with her. It was all as accessible to him as it was for our sister. Be it because of his youth, being a boy, or just the way he was inclined, it all went in one ear and out the other.

Deidra got his attention. "Hey, Lucius, guess what."

"What...?"

"You're gonna be an uncle."

"I didn't do anythin'!" Lucius said, defensively.

"Silly, ya don't have to do anythin' to be an uncle. Ya just gotta have a sister who's gonna have a baby."

"Are you gonna have a baby?" he asked, sounding confused.

"No, I ain't gonna have no baby. I'm too young. Audean is havin' the baby."

"How do ya know?"

"I heard her talkin' with Mama and Papa."

Lucius seemed to have caught up with the conversation, at this point. "Who's the daddy?' he asked.

"It be the savage they got chained up in the barn."

Lucius shivering as he spoke, as if just the thought ruined his day. "The savage, ya say. I sure hope the baby ain't born with two heads, or somethin'.""

"Ya truly ignorant, just hope it don't come out looking nothin' like you."

"How can it look like me?" The prospect confused Lucius.

"Never mind, silly bones. Come with me. We gotta help Audean."

"How...?"

"We goin' to the barn."

Lucius' shivers intensified.

"His name is Ku-jen-ga," Deidra announced, pronouncing each syllable slowly and clearly.

"I heard tell he's eats children," Lucius warned.

"Ya got nothin' to worry about. You'd probably taste so bad, he'd spit ya out."

The barn door was ajar. The two small children didn't even have to open the door, slipping in through the gap.

Kujenga jumped to his feet. He looked at them, intensely. He'd learn to trust nobody, even children.

"Howdy," Deidra said, smiling, slowly walking forward.

"Don't get to close," Lucius cautioned, walking close behind.

"I'm Deidra," she said, pointing to herself. "This here's Lucius," she said, pointing to her brother.

Kujenga gave no response.

"We be Audean's brother and sister," Lucius added.

A response flared in Kujenga, as his eyes went wide. "Audean...?" he questioned.

"That's right," Deidra said. "Audean..."

She had his full attention, but now what to do with it.

Deidra continued, despite the language barrier, hoping some of it would come across. "I figured we best meet, since we're all goin' to be family."

Lucius remained hidden behind his sister, his head peering out. "Dang, he's even bigger than what folks been sayin'," he whispered just loud enough for Deidra to hear.

"Audean...?" Kujenga asked once more, a hopeful note in his voice.

"That's right," Deidra said, "Audean." She's gonna have your baby."

She could see she wasn't getting her point across. She placed her hands a foot in front of her, rubbing an imaginary belly. "Baby...Audean...havin' your baby."

Still, there was no clear understanding by Kujenga.

Deidra folded her arms in front of her as if holding a baby. She rocked her arms back and forth, mimicking a baby crying. Then she'd rub her outstretched imaginary belly, again, and then rock the make-believe baby. She did these actions several times, all the while repeating, "Audean...baby...your baby."

In an instant, Kujenga's face lit up, smiling. He, too, rocked a pretend baby in his arms. "Matoto....Audean...Matoto?"

"That's right, Audean's havin' your baby," Deidra agreed.

"Matoto...Audean...Matoto wangu."

"That's right," Deidra smiled.

Kujenga burst into laughter, his voice filled with joy.

"He ain't very smart," Lucius whispered to his sister.

Even at her young age, Deidra was forming her likes and dislikes. "Smart...? Not in words, maybe. But I tell ya. If I told a man I was havin' his baby and he acted like that, I'd love him forever."

Ten

Never You Mind

It was true. I was in the family way, to everyone's disappointment, except Gethen. He was ecstatic. It fit in perfectly with his plan. He came rushing into the kitchen to congratulate me.

"Gossip grows faster than cotton on this plantation," he said, laughingly. "I heard you're with child. That's wonderful. I'm glad you finally came to your senses. You know, I only punished you for disobeying me. If you'd done it my way from the beginning, we'd still be where we are now, only you wouldn't have gotten a whooping."

I remember I was standing at the table cutting onions. I'm sure he took this as the reason for my watering eyes.

"Sir," I said with as much respect as I could muster. "I do care for this. It wasn't the way I'd want it to be, but it is the way it is. I beg ya, please, sir, let us marry?"

Gethen laughed so loud and hard the pots and pans rattled.

"Are you serious? Marry…? This is just the beginning. I plan to match him with every young girl on the plantation. He's going to sire a whole new generation of workers. No, girl, you may be the first, but you ain't the last. I'm going to get my money's worth out of him, tenfold. And if you could ask that savage, I'm sure he wouldn't complain." He turned to leave. "You take care of yourself and your baby, you hear, girl?"

When he was gone, I broke down in tears. Mama rushed to me, taking me in her arms.

"Never ya mind, child, never ya mind."

****

Her name was Deloris Haze, but everyone called her Dolly. She was a year older than me, a bit larger in everyway. She was pretty with a large dose of womanhood, if you catch my drift. She'd learned at an early age that beauty was power. She wheeled her good looks like a two-edged sword, one edge for attacking, the other for defense.

Let me explain what I mean by attacking and defense. You see, Dolly was a truly lazy person, always looking for the easy and most profitable path in life.

Understand, Dolly wasn't an evil person. She'd never go out of her way to hurt anyone. Though if someone got in her way or an opportunity should raise its head, no one would put it past her to do something unethical.

She knew how to wrap a man around her finger. Once a young man was in that position, he would do her bidding to the death. I'm not just talking about the young black men of the plantation. Folks knew she fraternized with some of the white overseers, as well. In short, Dolly did the minimum of work for the highest yield. She seldom wanted for anything, within reason; she *was* still a slave.

As for defense, she got away with murder. If something were missing from the main house, say one of madam's handkerchiefs or food from the kitchen, Dolly was the last to be questioned, if spoken to at all. And don't dare get on her bad side. Make an enemy of Dolly, and you've made many enemies.

As for our relationship, it was more of an acquaintance. Dolly and I never held a conversation. All words kept down to a minimum, such as "Good morning" or "Good night", which was just the way I preferred it, I assumed she felt the same. For this reason, it surprised me she'd seek out my friendship, taking me into her confidence, asking for my advice.

One night when Mama planned to stay late working at the main house, I walked home alone. It was already dark, so I moved slowly and carefully. When out of nowhere, Dolly appeared at my side. I nearly jumped out of my skin.

"Dolly, ya scared the bejeezus outta me!"

"Sorry, I was hiding in the bushes, waitin' for ya."

"What for…?"

"I need to talk with ya."

It took me off guard, but she had my curiosity.

"I need to get home," I said. "Walk with me." Once we started our pace, I asked her straight out, "So, what's so important that ya gotta talk with me?"

"It's about Kujenga," she said softly, looking around to be sure no one was listening.

I must admit, when I heard her say his name, my mind flooded with emotion. First, I was angry. How did she know his name? Then there was fear, afraid under Gethen's order she had slept with Kujenga.

"What about him?" I asked, coyly.

"Everybody knows ya havin' his baby."

I didn't answer, not confirming or denying. I continued walking.

"Massa Gethen locked me in the barn with him a few nights, now. Gethen tells me he wants me to have Kujenga's baby."

Still, I remained in silence, waiting for the other shoe to drop. Finally, when I couldn't bear feeling jealous any longer, I stopped and confronted her.

"What's this all gotta do with me?" I asked, sharply.

"He won't touch me. I spent every night for nearly a week in that barn, but Kujenga won't touch me."

My first emotion was relief, yet the more I thought about it, I realized it could turn into something dangerous for Dolly or even Kujenga.

"What can I do about that?" I snapped back.

"Ya havin' his baby, ain't ya? What'd ya do? I couldn't get him goin' in that direction. He even ignored me! Then I made the mistake of mentioning your name. He kept sayin' over and over, 'Audean...Audean.' He just sat there staring at the ground, looking like he was gonna cry."

I can't tell you how light my heart grew at hearing this.

"Tell me, what is ya secret?" Dolly asked, sounding surprised, for I knew she thought much of herself and little of me.

I shook my head, laughing.

"What be so funny?" Dolly asked in anger.

"Ya just don't get it, do ya?" I said, still shaking my head.

"Get what?"

"That there might be somethin' between Kujenga and me."

Now, it was Dolly's turn to laugh. "Ya just don't know men," she shot back. Then she went solemn. "Audean, ya just gotta help me. If I don't turn up with a belly, soon, I don't know what Massa Gethen gonna do to me."

I could tell her fear and concern were genuine. I stopped shaking my head. "I don't know what to tell ya, Dolly. I'm sorry," I said with much feeling for her. I pitied her, but was serious; I had no answer for her. I could feel her eyes on the back of me as I walked away toward home.

****

Dolly was far more resourceful than I ever took her to be. In a few weeks, she turned up in the family way.

At first, I felt disheartened to learn this. The thought, perhaps, Dolly had worn down Kujenga's resistance. After all, she knew men better than I did. Maybe, love isn't enough. I was heartbroken, until I learned the truth.

Yes, she was with child, only the talk in the slave's quarters told the facts she was carrying the baby of Kendal Morris, a handsome black man, considered a catch for any black woman on the plantation.

Dolly's plan was to pass off Kendal's child as the child of Kujenga. This she hoped would appease Massa Gethen.

But there was a very large fly in this ointment. As Gethen pointed out, gossip was the fastest growing crop on the plantation. Considering that, there is one fact that needs clarification.

Often, when most folk hear the word *Gossip*, they think of women, especially white haired old biddies with nothing but time on their hands, their nose in everybody else's business. This is an imbalanced view. In my years, I've known many men with big mouths. Such is the case of Kendal Morris.

For many of the young men on the plantation, both black and white, Dolly was considered a great prize. I don't understand why, since she was so easily won. Once Kendal had been with Dolly, he set into bragging up a storm to anyone who'd listen – mostly men. These men reveled in the dirt, passing it on every chance they got.

In no time, the chain of gossip ended with Furcas Gethen. He was upset, to say the least. Mostly, he was angry with Dolly for lying to him. Her punishment was the removal of all the perks in her life. From that day on, Dolly would have to work for a living, just like all the other slaves. As for Kendal, not much changed, his life was never easy, Gethen made sure that never changed.

There is one part of Dolly's story that hurt me deeply. Because of her condition, Dolly and Kendal received permission to wed. For me, this was only a dream for Kujenga and me that I feared would never come true.

Eleven

Saint Erasmus

The Dolly fiasco did not discourage Gethen. Nothing could sway him from his plan. He began scheduling different young slave girls, six girls in all, to spend the night in the barn with Kujenga. Gethen believed that in time some or all would be in the family way. However, the story had an underbelly no one dared speak of.

It seems that every one of the six girls failed. For whatever reason, be it a mutual agreement between the girl and Kujenga, or just his grounds, but nothing ever happened. Some of the girls were too modest for such a relationship. They would remain fully dressed, seated on the ground, smiling at Kujenga, he smiling at them. Others, like Dolly, who were not as reserved, Kujenga turned down their advances.

I had mixed feelings. It pleased me to learn that Kujenga remained true, other than that, I knew it would mean trouble, both for him and the girls.

You see, each girl feared the wrath of Gethen. When night after night, nothing occurred, they kept it a secret to themselves, never telling a soul, neither family nor friend.

Gethen didn't suspect a fly in the ointment until weeks passed and there was no word from any of the girls that they'd been successful. He knew the problem wasn't with Kujenga. After all, I was without a doubt heavy with child. My profile was crescent moon shaped.

One by one, they ushered each girl to Gethen's library to be interrogated by him. His larger than life demeanor, bullish ways, and booming voice, frightened each one to confess that none of them ever knew Kujenga – in the Biblical sense, that is. All of them not only confessed but burst into tears, some of them falling to their knees, begging for leniency.

Realizing Kujenga was the problem, Gethen needed a way to get the upper hand. Strangely enough, the answer concerned both my mother and father.

Fearing her cooking would come into blame, my mother reported to Massa Gethen that Kujenga was refusing his food. All his meals came back to the kitchen untouched. I knew why, I, too, found my heart hungrier than my stomach.

When questioned, my father admitted every meal he brought to the barn he returned intact.

This gave Gethen an idea. He ordered my mother to stop making plates up for Kujenga and for my father to deliver to the barn only one mug of water, each day.

Gethen didn't want Kujenga to die, that would defeat the purpose. However, he did want him to suffer enough to change his ways.

A week went by, there seemed to be no change in Kujenga. Perhaps, his fortitude was stronger than most. The Bible talks about fasting in the wilderness for forty days. Surely, no man could withstand more.

When weeks passed, and Kujenga's health seemed the same, Gethen became suspicious. He called my mother and father to the library for questioning.

"Mary...Joseph, I'm going to ask this just once. I want a truthful answer." He looked to my mother. "Mary, have you been sending meals to the boy in the barn?"

"Massa Gethen, I would never do that. Ya said not to and I don't."

"You know, Mary, if you're lying, I'll find out."

"Why would I do that, Massa Gethen? That boy don't mean nothin' to me."

Gethen gave her a hard stare before dismissing her. "You can go back to the kitchen, Mary. I want to talk with your husband."

When she'd left, Gethen stood face-to-face with my father, looking coldly into his eyes.

"Joseph...the same question, have you been sneaking food to that boy after I told you not to?"

Papa stared right back at Gethen.

"No, sir, I only brings him water once a day like ya told me. If it were up to me...." Papa stopped midsentence when he realized he was overstepping his bounds.

"Go ahead, Joseph. If it were up to you, what would you do? I'm curious to know. Go ahead; I won't hold it against you. I'd like to hear this."

Papa hesitated for a moment, and then spoke slowly. "If it were up to me, I wouldn't even give him water. I'd let him die of thirst, if it were up to me. In fact, if I had my druthers, I'd go into that barn, right now, and kill him dead."

Gethen smiled. The idea of such hatred gave him pleasure.

"Really...?" Gethen asked laughingly. "And why is that?"

"Because of what he did to my daughter, sir, she's havin' that monster's baby. Ain't nothin' good gonna come from it. I wish that boy was dead and he can take his baby with him straight to hell."

Gethen burst into laughter, fully amused. "Well, I'm afraid that's just not going to happen. But, I'll tell you what. Not giving him water sounds like a good idea. From now on, until I tell you otherwise, don't bring him any water as well as food. Let's see how long he can hold out."

❊❊❊❊❊❊❊

Days passed, it would seem Kujenga's will was stronger than Gethen expected. He personally went into the barn to see for himself. Kujenga looked no worse for wear. He was as strong as ever.

When Gethen entered the barn, Kujenga rose to a standing position. Gethen kept his distance, moving in just enough to get a good look, estimating the condition of his property. That was when their eyes met.

Kujenga didn't need to speak the language; he instinctively knew who stood before him, the man behind his misery – his capture – his enemy. Kujenga's eyes were like daggers burrowing their way into Gethen's soul. He stood naked, ashamed, from this heathen's stare. It made him so uncomfortable; he rushed out of the barn.

Safely back in his library, Gethen summoned Hackett, the head overseer.

"Hackett, someone is sneaking food and water to that savage in the barn, after I gave strict orders for him to go without. It's been a week, and he looks as healthy as a horse. I'm fairly sure it's none of the house staff or the slave Joseph who was bringing him meals. At first, I though it might be Joseph's daughter, that Audean girl. After all, she is carrying his baby. I've watched her closely. After the whipping she got the last time she disobeyed, she'd never try anything like that again. She's got too much to risk, with the baby, and all. No, it's someone we least expect."

"Why don't we just put a lock on the barn door? That should stop whoever's doin' this," Hackett offered.

"I thought of that," Gethen replied. "It would seem the most logical thing to do. Only, if we do, we'd never catch the culprit. No, I want to catch this person red-handed. I want their hide. I want to make an example of them, so no one will ever try a stunt like this again."

"I understand, Mr. Gethen," Hackett agreed. "I'll have some of the boys watch the barn during the night."

"When you find out who it is, don't hold them. Let them go back to their home. Let me know who it is; I'll take care of them."

"Yes, sir," Hackett nodded understanding, heading for the library door.

"Oh, Hackett," Gethen called out.

"Yes, sir," Hackett turned, standing in the doorway.

"When we catch this person, I want them punished in front of all the slaves on the plantation. It's got to be something so horrible; it'll burn in their memories. Something that will put the fear of the devil in them, the Saint Erasmus death should do it."

"Yes, sir," answered Hackett, cringing as he left. He knew what the death of Saint Erasmus entailed; it made him shiver.

****

Hackett had some of the overseers move a wagon a few feet from the front of the barn, placing a large green tarp over it. After sunset, Hackett ordered his men to break up in teams of two. They would take three-hour shifts throughout the night on the wagon, covered by the tarp, keeping watch over the barn door. When the first shift was to come to a close, one of the men watching would wake the next two watchers, and they'd switch places. This way everyone got at least some sleep, and it assured that whoever was on watch would be alert. They all knew that if they fell asleep on the job it would mean their jobs, so they took it all very seriously.

It was during the fourth watch, just after one in the morning, there was a stir in the night. The two overseers hiding in the wagon peered from under the tarp.

A single small figure slowly opened the barn door and entered.

"Could ya see who it was?" one of the overseers whispered to the other.

"Nay, it's too damn dark to see. His back was to us, anyways. We'll get a better look at him when he comes out."

A few minutes later, the barn door opened slightly. The same small figure shimmied out through the slim opening, holding an empty dinner plate and cup.

"It's a man, for sure, but I can't make out his face," the overseer said in a low voice.

There was only a quarter-moon in the night sky, giving off just enough light to make out shapes, nothing more. Gradually, the figure stepped away from the barn, out from the shadow of the overhang. The moon's dull glow struck his face, illuminating it.

"I'll be damned! It's Gloomy! Why that foxy old man, do ya believe it?"

"Remember what Hackett said. The boss don't want us to do anything about it, just make a report in the mornin'."

As they climbed out from the back of the wagon, dusting off their clothes, they shook their heads, giggling.

"Gethen's gonna take it out on Gloomy, for sure."

"Yeah, I pity the old man."

Pity or not, it didn't stop them from laughing.

✷✸✷✸✷✸✷

The sound of the bell shattered the morning. They walked from the slave quarters to the main house in fear. All knew what was to come, one of their own facing punishment. The penalty would be paid in flesh, the amount determined by the weight of the infraction, anywhere from whipping, to mutilation, or even death.

With sorrowful faces the crowd of slaves stood before the main house. Something was different. There were no horses, wagon, or rope. This would not be a hanging. None of the overseers carried a whip. There would not be a lashing. A single wooden stump stood knee-height in the center of the clearing.

Gethen walked down from the porch, standing before them. He wore riding boots and held a riding crop in his hand. Without saying a word, his wishes made law. He nodded to Hackett. The next instant, they shoved Gloomy into the clearing. The old man fell to the ground at Gethen's feet.

"All of you know why we're here. We've been here before. You're asking yourself, 'What did Gloomy do? What could an old man do that would call for punishment?'"

Gethen waited a moment to be sure he held their attention.

"I strictly forbid anyone to give food or drink to the savage in the barn. Gloomy disobeyed. Now, Gloomy must pay."

Gethen looked to the overseers. "Hackett, go into the barn, bring the savage out. He needs to see this more than anyone. He might not speech English, but he'll understand what he's been a part of and who rules this plantation."

Hackett ran off, entering the barn. Everyone waited in silence. Gethen looked into their eyes, one by one, purposely to intimidate them. Gloomy remained on the ground, looking forlorn, staring into the dust.

Gethen looked to the barn door, anticipating Hackett exiting with the savage in tow by the chain around his neck. An unreasonable amount of time passed with no sign of Hackett and the savage. Gethen was just about to order one of the overseers to go into the barn to see what the delay was when Hackett flew out of the barn. He ran to the clearing, standing between Gethen and Gloomy. He was out of breath, his face was flushed. Gethen said not a word, staring at Hackett, his stern look demanding an answer.

"He ain't there!" Hackett blurred out.

"What do you mean he's not there?" Gethen growled "He was chained up!"

Hackett took in a deep breath. "The chain's been cut. He ain't there!" Hackett stepped forward, pointing to the overseers. "We can be after him within the hour."

"Wait!" Gethen ordered, raising his palm for everything to halt. "Our business, here, is not finished, yet." Gethen walked forward, standing over Gloomy. He pressed his boot down on Gloomy's hand. Gloomy screamed in pain.

"What did you do, old man," Gethen asked, pressing his boot down harder.

Gloomy wriggled on the ground. His head went back. He cried through gritted teeth. "I ain't done nothin', sir. I fed him, but I ain't cut no chains."

Gethen pressed his boot harder on the old man's hand, until he was sure Gloomy was telling the truth.

"Mr. Hackett, you know what to do," Gethen said, backing away from the clearing toward the main house. He shouted so all could hear. "I want all of you to watch and learn what happens to anyone who disobeys. If I catch anyone not watching, I'll have your eye plucked out. Watch and learn." Gethen stepped up onto the porch to get a better view.

Two overseers lifted Gloomy from off the ground, holding him up, one on each side. Standing in front of Gloomy, Hackett tore the shirt off the old man, throwing the tattered cloth to the ground. No one had any idea how frail Gloomy was. His body was nothing more than bones wrapped around by paper-thin skin. His ribs were like stripes with a furrow between them deep enough to stick your thumb in.

Reaching down, Hackett pulled a long knife from the inside of his boot.

There was a tension in the air that everyone breathe in, settling heavy within the lungs, causing a tight strangle grip around their hearts.

Hackett brought the blade in closer to Gloomy. With one quick jab he could kill the old man, but that was not the plan.

The death of Saint Erasmus is a slow, agonizing death; bringing the victim to the point where they beg for the mercy of death. Saint Erasmus: The third century monk from Italy, the patron saint of sailors, children with colic, intestinal ailments and diseases, cramps, and the pain of women in labor.

Bringing the blade in close, Hackett neither stabbed nor jabbed, but slowly cut the layer of skin of Gloomy's right side, just below the ribcage. The wound was a long, thin, vertical red line. Hackett pushed the wound open with the tip of his knife until it was a wide opening in the old man's side. With his free hand, Hackett reached into the wound, pulling out Gloomy's intestines, inch by inch until he held enough in his hand to tie around the post that was in the center of the clearing.

Gasps, screams filled the air. Women fell to the ground in a faint. I reached out to someone next to me, placing my hand on their shoulder to brace myself. Damn Gethen's threats, I closed my eyes, unable to watch.

Above all the shrieks, I heard Gloomy howling in pain. Finally, when I just had to see what was happening, I opened my eyes. Gloomy was shouting to heaven as he walked around the post, his entrails wrapping around the wooden stake in the ground. Each time he walked a full-length around, another foot of his bowels was pulled from his side.

Then it happened, the moment of Gethen's complete victory over the will of another man, when Gloomy could take it no more, pleading for mercy.

"Kill me... somebody, please, kill me!" he shouted over and over, but it was not to be. He was destined for a long, slow, painful death.

They dismissed everyone; mother and I went to the kitchen of the main house to cook the meals for the Gethen family. The others were off to the field. For nearly six hours, we could hear Gloomy's screams. I'm sure they heard him out in the fields. It was like a heavy weight pressing down on you, making everything difficult.

Being in my condition, Mama took pity on me. She sat me down at the kitchen table while she did all the work, preparing the meals. We didn't speak, moving about slowly, like ghosts.

There was little to do, fewer cooking than most days, just the meals of the madam of the house and her children. All the others, Gethen and his men, rode off as soon as we were dismissed. They rode off to hunt down the savage, my Kujenga. Only a few overseers remained, just enough to insure everyone put in a full day's work in a peaceful manner.

There would be no rebellion. Fear flowed through our veins, mixing with our blood. Our hearts and lungs pumping like steam engines.

Finally, thank God, Gloomy's cries stopped. He was dead. At last, he received the mercy he pleaded six hours for.

Twelve

In The Wilderness

Hackett took no chances. Before the ordeal with Gloomy, he ordered some of the overseers to get the horses ready for the hunt of the savage.

The Gethen Plantation was acres arranged in a circle of cotton fields surrounded on all sides by deep woods. They broke up into four groups with Gethen taking the group going north, Hackett taking a group going south, the two most likely directions. Beyond the forest were other plantations. Gethen ordered four of his men to race to his neighbors, telling them of the situation. Though all plantation owners were in competition, in such matters they had one another's backs. This forced Kujenga to stay within the surrounding forest. Once he stepped out into the open, all would be lost.

I worried for Kujenga. It all seemed hopeless. However, the tension eased up when Gethen and his men returned that evening without Kujenga. I even experienced a feeling of optimism when after four days they still had no luck.

From his years as a boy in Africa, Kujenga learned to survive in the jungle. In many ways, a forest is similar to a jungle, the trees are different; the animals are different, but if you can survive in a jungle, you can surely survive in a forest. Though Kujenga would be vulnerable beyond that point, within he could survive indefinitely. After a week with no sign of Kujenga, Gethen realized he'd need another strategy.

"Take this letter to Sherman," Gethen ordered Hackett, handing him an envelope.

Gregg Sherman was a neighboring plantation owner. His spread wasn't near as large or as fine as Gethen's, nor did he have as many slaves or overseers, but he did have one thing Gethen wished he had. That was Charley One Horse of the Cheyenne Nation. He was a squatty little man with dark skin, his hair in braids. He wore an old British officer's jacket that his grandfather acquired during the revolutionary war. A long string of beads around his neck, he always wore moccasins. Sherman kept Charley on hand, at great expense. Charley was famous for is ability to track down any stray animal or runaway slave. He was worth his weight in gold, and Sherman knew it. Gethen's letter was a request to borrow Charley to track down Kujenga. Sherman agreed, but at a hefty price, paid in full, in advance, with no refunds, no matter what the outcome. Gethen was at a loss. There was nothing to do but to agree to the terms.

Charley One Horse received free rein over the Gethen Plantation; he could question anyone and inspect anyplace. He started with the barn, spending nearly an hour giving it more than the once-over. He was seen hovering low to the ground all around the main house, the slave quarters, the overseers' quarters, the fields, and of course, in the surrounding forest. Everyone thought it all very strange; still, they figured he knew what he was doing. Finally, he made his first report to Gethen.

"He's held up in the woods to the north of your property."

"You're sure he's still in the woods?" Gethen asked.

"I've checked the land beyond there, I'm sure of it. He's still in the woods. Besides, I saw signs he's there. He's been wandering, living on berries and root, as well as fish from the stream and small animals he set traps for."

This puzzled Gethen. "How could that be? We haven't seen any smoke from a campfire."

"He's eatin' 'em raw," One Horse replied.

This made Gethen's stomach turn. He shivered at just the thought.

"A man's gotta do what a man's gotta do," One Horse stated. "We're dealing with a man who knows how to hide and how to survive in the wilderness. Still, if ya give me about four or five men, I'm sure we could flush him out."

****

Charley One Horse, with Gethen and five of his men, entered the forest, not emerging for a week. They returned tired, hungry, and empty-handed. It was a strange ability Kujenga possessed to be able to elude One Horse, one of the finest trackers in the state. Understandably, this disappointed Gethen, only more so than one would imagine. His arrangement with Gregg Sherman was a large sum for the loan of Charley One Horse. Nothing was mentioned about results. Win or lose, capture the savage or not, the sum must be paid in full. This chafed Gethen to no end. However, when Gethen was lost for a course of strategy, a stranger showed up at his doorstep, guaranteeing results.

"There's a man here to see ya, sir," announced Gethen's manservant as he entered the library.

"Who is it? What does he want?" Gethen asked, not looking up from his desk, writing in his accounting ledger.

"Don't rightly know, sir, only he says he's a tracker."

"Tell him I've had my fill of Indian trackers."

"Oh, he ain't no Indian, sir."

Gethen looked up from his work. "He isn't; then what is he?"

"Couldn't say, sir, he be a strange looking sort."

This perked Gethen's interest.

"Very well, show him in."

It was true. The man who entered the library was different from anyone Gethen ever knew. Not only as to what he wore, which Gethen thought was strange, but in his physical appearance, as well as his mannerisms.

He was a young man, in his twenties. Save for his cotton white shirt, everything was leather, his boots, his pants, his jacket, all the way up to his horsehide hat, wide-brimmed of black and white pinto hide.

His head closely shaven, as was his face and eyebrows. His eyes were dark, nearly black. His skin had a different hue to it, what most folk would call olive – a deep olive color.

Gethen remained seated behind his desk, giving the stranger the once-over.

"So, you're a tracker?" Gethen finally asked. "Who sent you?"

"Nobody," the stranger replied. "They say you've lost a very expensive slave."

"*They* do talk a lot, don't *they*?"

"I can find him for you and bring him back, and you won't have to pay me until I bring him in."

"And what is your price for his capture and return?"

"Five hundred dollars..."

"A bit steep, don't you think?"

"It's well worth it, and you know it. As I was saying, there is no payment until results."

"I have to ask," Gethen said, sounding amused. "Who are you, and what makes you think you can do better than the others."

"My name is Treven Gilley. I was born and raised in the jungles of Africa, just like your runaway. I know all he knows, I know all the tricks."

"How did you wind up in the South?"

"My mother was black, my father was white. My father died when I was a boy. My mother and I returned to her village, where I was raised. When she died, I decided to come to the Americas to seek my fortune."

"I thought there was something different about you," Gethen remarked. "I figure you for the darkest white man I've ever met."

Now, it was Treven who smiled. "That's odd. I've always thought of myself as a very light black man."

They both laughed, now that all the cards were laid on the table.

"Well, Mr. Gilley, I'm not very enthused about your price, still, I do like the terms. Since I've nothing to lose, I'm going to give you a chance. When can you start?"

"Immediately..."

"How long will it take?"

"Perhaps a few weeks..."

"A few weeks…!" Gethen said, startled.

"Mr. Gethen, let me explain. I suspect this is no ordinary black slave from Africa. In his village, he was probably an important man, a warrior. He's been trained since he was a boy to survive in the wilderness. He knows how to fight. He's doubtlessly very smart and very dangerous."

"How many men will you need?" asked Gethen.

"I'll go after him alone. When I have a good idea where he's hiding, I'll return. That's when I'll need at least five men to bring him in."

The two went silent for a moment, considering all that was said.

"Well, Mr. Gethen, do we have a deal?" Treven asked, holding out his hand, clearly wanting to seal the deal with a handshake.

Gethen rose, walking to Treven. His movements were slow. He hesitated to shake Traven's hand. Not because he questioned the arrangement, remembering he had nothing to lose. It was just now Gethen looked on Treven as a black man. He was not used to making deals with black men, let alone shaking their hands. But the deal was good, better than a jab in the eye with a sharp stick.

The two shook hands, giving each other an icy stare.

"Mr. Gethen, I will see you in one to three weeks."

Treven turned, leaving the room. When the sound of his boots on the wooden floor stopped, signifying he'd left the main house, Gethen looked out the back window. He watched Treven Gilley walk across the far cotton fields, disappearing into the woods at the far north.

||*|*|*|*|*

Ten days passed since Treven Gilley made his bold statement in the library to Gethen. It was a quiet afternoon, working in the kitchen with my mother, when we heard the front door of the main house, open and slam close. Treven Gilley stormed into the house, unannounced, walking straight to the library. He must have had good news for Gethen to be so bold. I stepped out in the hall. I could hear the entire conversation.

"Mr. Gilley, I don't approve of you crashing in like this," Gethen said, sitting at his desk.

"I found him," Treven announced, which was all he need say to change Gethen's mood. Gethen broke out in a smile.

"That's good. Where do have him? Bring him to me."

Treven nonchalantly walked closer, plopping down in one of the chairs in front of the desk.

"I said I found him. I didn't say I captured him. This man is a warrior, very dangerous. I'm going to need at leash five of your best men to bring him in."

"I'll have Hackett get on it immediately."

Treven raised his palms to Gethen to halt him.

"Hold your horses, Mr. Gethen. It's late in the day. The sun is beginning to set. By the time they get ready and we entered the forest, it'll be night, too dark to do anything. Just tell your men to be ready with the first light. Tell them to pack enough food for a week."

"You think it will take that long?" Gethen asked.

"I wouldn't be surprise. This man we're after is no ordinary man. In the meantime, I'd like to get something to eat and someplace were I can rest up."

"Of course...of course..." Gethen said, eagerly rising and walking to the closed library door. Treven stood up. "Just go through this door, go down the hall, the kitchen is on your right. Have the girls make you something."

"And a place to sleep...?"

"I'll have Hackett set you up in the barn. I'm afraid I can't offer you a room here in my house, under the circumstance, you being what you are, and all. You do understand?"

"Fully, sir," Treven replied. "I wouldn't think of spending a night under the same roof as you and your family." Funny, the way Treven said this; it was not in a tone of someone insulted, but one of someone making an insult.

I rushed back down the hall and into the kitchen. I heard the library door open and close and Treven's boots in the hall. The kitchen door opened, he entered. Standing in the center of the room, he looked at both my mother and me.

"The boss tells me I can get something to eat, here."

"What would ya like?" my mother asked.

"Vegetables, whatever you have, only no meat, please."

"No meat?" Mama questioned. "Do ya eat eggs?"

"No eggs, please..."

"No eggs," Mama echoed in disappointment. "I can boil ya up whatever vegetables I got and serve 'em with bread and butter."

"That would be fine, only no butter, please."

At least he was polite.

"What would ya like to drink?"

"Water would be fine, thank you."

"Audean, go out to the pump and fetch this man some fresh water."

He ate in silence. I positioned myself behind him, watching his every move. Holding a pitcher of water, I approached him.

"Would ya care for more water, sir?" I asked.

"Yes, please," he said, holding out his mug for me to fill.

That was when our eyes met. He looked me over, his gaze settling on my now plump belly.

"You're carrying his child, aren't you?"

Afraid to say a word, I just nodded.

"Don't worry. I'm just going to bring him in. No ones going to harm him."

Somehow, his words comforted me.

He rose from the table, heading toward the back door.

"That was all very nice, ladies. I thank you, both. You have a good day."

And then he left.

We watched from the window, watching him walk away, wondering what sort of man was he.

After cleaning up, I took an old sack and began filling it with whatever food I could fit in it.

"What are ya doin', child?" Mama asked.

"I'm goin' to the woods to warn Kujenga."

"Girl, ya ain't in no condition to be trampin' through no woods."

Standing in the doorway with the sack slung over my shoulder, I looked directly into my mother's face.

"You'd do it for Papa, if ya had to."

She had no answer for this. She knew in her heart I was right.

"Don't tell anyone what I've done."

She nodded.

"I love ya, Mama," I said as I left, closing the door behind me.

I heard her mournful voice call to me through the door. "I love ya, too, child. God be with ya."

Thirteen

With No Dreams

I understood my mother's concern the moment I stepped out of the fields and into the woods. The overhead branches blocked out the sun. The ground was a problem, walking was difficult. The rocks and stones jutted out every few inches, while the roots of trees entwined, some six inches high or more. I was in no condition to make such a journey. I kept reminding myself that if I stumbled and fell, to make like a cat, flipping my body so I'd land on my back or side. Any which way to protect my swollen belly where rested my child – Kujenga and mine, that is.

Despite the danger, I trudge on, knowing in my heart I was doing what was right. I needed to find Kujenga before the search party did. I had a few hours head start. However, my condition was sure to slow me down, and their determination would quickly close that gap.

What worried me most was the way Treven Gilley spoke to Massa Gethen, when I listened in, standing outside the library. He sounded so sure of himself. The man was confident he could deliver on his promises.

My strength came in spurts; I tired easily, stopping often to regain my wind. I'd walk a quarter mile, needing to stop. Each rest period was longer than the one before, as my vigor faded.

Midafternoon, I stopped for something to eat. Figuring, the hard-boiled egg in my sack would be the first item to go bad, I ate it with a sliver of bread. The dryness of it all made me thirsty. That's when I heard it, the sound of running water not far away. I walked to it. Pushing away a tall bush, I saw a thin stream. The water ran fast, meaning it was fresh. I got down on my knees, cupped my hands, bringing water to my mouth. As I drank, I looked at the silt a few inches below the moving water. It was the unmistakable impression of a foot. From the width and depth of it, I knew it was Kujenga's footprint. I was glad, knowing I was on the right path. Still, it gave me pause. If I, not being a tracker, could find such a clue to Kujenga's whereabouts, how much more would Treven Gilley be able to hunt him down? I could only hope, Kujenga left it on purpose to throw them off his trail.

The rest of the day was hard on me. I traveled slower with each hour. Early evening, between the overhead foliage blocking out the sky and the sun setting over the horizon, darkness closed in around me. When moving became nearly impossible, I found a massive tree with two large roots that formed a V-shape. I sat on the ground, my back to the trunk. I ate the last crust of bread with a piece of dry beef.

There comes a time in everyone's life when all seems too big to handle, completely out of your hands. At those times, some folks give up and run away, or live their life under a cloud of hopelessness, pretending it never happened. As well, some folks fight it, become overwhelmed, and then go mad. I never was the praying type, but I knew I was powerless. I closed my eyes, praying for help from a God I barely knew. I had to. I was alone, feeling helpless.

It was no comfort, at first. Then when sleep took me, I dreamed. In that dream, I saw Kujenga standing before me. I knew it was a dream because I understood every word he said to me.

"Audean," he said, reaching out, taking my hand. "Audean, I've come halfway around the world to be with you. I love you. I always loved you, and I will forever love you."

I remember I was just about to say *I love you, too* when he pulled me in close, kissing me. His kiss was warm, strong, and comforting. I felt so protected in his arms.

Suddenly, I realized something was wrong. Standing so close to him, I couldn't feel my belly against him.

I backed away, screaming, my hand on my flat belly, "Our baby...where is our baby?"

"There's no baby," Kujenga said. "There's just you and me."

"There was a baby!" I shouted, feeling the emptiness inside me. "There was a baby, I swear there was!"

I woke, startled, shivering in a cold sweat. It was still night. There were tears in my eyes, as I put my hand on my belly, feeling it swollen with child. I felt it kicking inside me.

"It's all right, baby, it was just a dream," I whispered, closing my eyes, hoping never to dream, again.

****

Rays of sunlight sifting through the canopy of leaves, danced over my eyes, waking me with the morning light. I felt rested, stronger. I began heading north. The ground under my feet began to slope upwards. In time, the steepness grew. I was definitely traveling up hill. Eventually, there were fewer trees, as I approached the summit. When I got to the top, I stood looking back. I was high enough to see for miles. There were the miles of the forest that I had traveled. Beyond that I could see on the horizon the Gethen Plantation.

Looking south, a mile off, I saw something move. I waited and watched. Then I saw it again, just for a moment, the head of someone moving through the forest. It was Treven Gilley with Gethen's men. They were on foot.

I'm sure the head I saw was one of Gethen's men. Gilley would not be so careless. Moreover, believing Gilley to be as good at his job, I could only take for granted that if I could see them, he could see me. I turned, knowing I had to get as much distance between us as I could.

Coming over the crest, and then downhill, the trees became more and closer woven. I was back in the forest, again, into the dark woods.

Hurrying onward, I heard the sound of running water in the distance. This was different from the small creek I came on the day before. I knew it just by the sound of it. The rushing sound of waves hitting rocks grew louder as I approached. Coming out of the woods I was face-to-face with a running stream of water at least twenty feet wide. It didn't look like a far distance, nor did it look deep, except it was fast moving. I knew I didn't have much choice. If Kujenga was in the part of the forest from which I just passed, he would have come to me. Surely, he was somewhere beyond this stream. As well, Treven Gilley and Gethen's men were not far behind; perhaps, less than a mile. Also, I was sure they saw me, and were rushing towards me that very minute. There was nothing else for me than to forge the stream.

I would need the use of both my hands so I tossed my sack of food into the bushes. I dipped my right foot into the water. It was cold. Putting my other foot in, I walked forward until it was knee-deep. The force of the water was strong. Still, it was nothing I felt I couldn't handle. I gained confidence, moving forward.

When the water level was up to my hips, I realized I'd misjudged the power of the stream's flow. Except, it was too late, I tried turning back; the strength of the rushing water prevented me, knocked me down, taking me downstream.

My feet no longer touched bottom. I began spinning like a top. My head bobbed up and down with my face to the sky and then spinning underwater. I held my breath as best I could, praying to be spun around, again, to get a full breath, only to be pushed below the waterline to hold my breath, once more.

With a shock, I began crashing into rocks that jutted out from the water. My first reaction was to bring my hands up to cover my face. Then I remembered my child, my first responsibility. I wrapped my arms around my belly, protecting my baby.

With my face and head exposed, I went head on, face first into the rocks. It all happened so fast, there wasn't time to feel any pain. Nonetheless, I knew something was desperately wrong when I tasted blood in my mouth. With each blow to my head, I began to lose consciousness. The world became blurry, faraway.

The current pulled me down. As everything became dark, I resolved to death. Suddenly, I felt a strong arm take hold of me, lifting me to the surface. I was sure it was my guardian angel taking my soul to heaven. Coming up, I filled my lungs with sweet air. The breath went to my head. Just before I passed out, I looked into the face of my redeemer. It was Kujenga.

****

It wasn't a dream. When I came to, I felt like I was floating. I opened my eyes. I was in Kujenga's arms.

"Kujenga," I whispered.

He smiled at me, shushing me to relax. I let him carry me.

Looking up at the sun, I realized we were heading back to the Gethen Plantation.

"Kujenga, ya mustn't do this. I don't need help. I'll be fine."

Again, he shushed me.

It was true. I wasn't well. All the pain that I should have felt when I hit those rocks in the water, now, flooded over me. Looking at my hands, I saw blood. Kujenga's hands were covered in blood, as were my clothes. I closed my eyes, letting go.

Still in Kujenga's arms, I woke to the sound of voices. I looked to see Treven Gilley and Gethen's men rushing us.

"Kaa huko," Gilley shouted, bringing his rifle up, pointing it at Kujenga.

Obviously, Kujenga understood what was said, stopping in his tracks.

One of them took me away from Kujenga. The others rushed him, tying his hands behind him, while Gilley held his rifle on him. Kujenga didn't put up a struggle. He knew it would be useless to not comply. Still, he looked content, knowing I would be taken to the plantation where I'd get help. My safety was his only concern.

It was a slow march back to the plantation, as I needed to be carried. The men took turns holding me in their arms. They kept Kujenga out front where they could watch his every move. Gilley walked behind him, holding a rifle, never taking his aim off him.

Arriving at the plantation, there was a lot of confusion, people running around. I was too weak, falling in and out of consciousness to make any sense of it. All I remember was them taking me to my home, placing me on my bed where I immediately fell into a deep sleep, a sleep, thank God, with no dreams.

Fourteen

No Tears Were Shed

Opening my eyes, I saw my mother's face looking down on me. I had no idea how much time passed. I suspected it was hours, as I was still in my bed. I was naked; my mother sitting on the edge of the bed, washing me. She stopped, placed the washcloth in a basin, turning, taking my hands in hers.

"Audean..." she said, stopping, her voice breaking. Tears ran down her face. "Audean...the baby....ya lost the baby."

There was a long moment of silence. A large gap between the world and me widened beyond my sight; my mother's words sounded far off. When they finally made it to my brain, I didn't cry, but shook as if I were struck with fever. My mouth wouldn't form words. The dream, that horrible dream in which Kujenga spoke English, telling me there was no baby, came true.

I didn't ask if it had been a boy or girl. I was afraid to know. Mama didn't volunteer that information. She was afraid to tell me.

Just as Mama covered me with a blanket, the bell in front of the main house sounded. Punishment to be dealt out, all forced to witness.

"I have to go," Mama whispered. "I'll be back as soon as I can."

Before she left the room, we heard a loud thud in the main room. Someone kicked our front door in. The bedroom door flew open. Hackett stood in the doorway, two other overseers stood behind him.

"Everyone needs to come to the main house," Hackett said, "including her."

"She's ill, she can't be moved," Mama protested.

"Orders is orders," Hackett replied.

"The poor girl can't even walk," Mama shouted.

Hackett hauled off hitting Mama with the back of his hand. She flew into the wall.

"The boss wants her there," Hackett insisted. "If she can't walk, we'll carry her." Hackett pointed to the overseers. "Go ahead, boys."

The two overseers picked me up off the bed. For modesty's sake, they left the blanket wrapped around me.

At the main house, someone took pity on me, putting a chair out for me. The overseers set me down on it.

Kujenga stood in the center of the clearing, his hands still bound behind his back. He looked about for a friendly face; there were none to be found, until his eyes met mine.

Even in the midst of all that surrounded us, we smiled at each other, finding peace in our gaze.

Gethen walked to the center of the clearing, standing next to Kujenga.

"It seems you have no friends among these people," Gethen told Kujenga, looking at him, though not understanding the words, yet comprehending the sentiment.

Gethen spoke loud, slowly, clearly, as if making a proclamation.

"All of you know why I brought this savage to my plantation. My plans have not been carried out, so far; nevertheless, they will be carried out. My will be done!" He shouted, sending a shiver through everyone, including the overseers. He continued, "This savage didn't submit to my plans. In fact, he ran off, avoiding my wishes. Now, I can't get into a man's head, stopping him from thinking the way he does. But I can make his plans useless. Keeping in mind what this savage is here for, I realized not all of his body parts are necessary to perform his duties."

Gethen backed away from Kujenga, out of the clearing, standing on the main house porch.

"Mr. Hackett, if you please," Gethen shouted.

Three overseers entered the clearing as Hackett went into the barn. Two of them each took one of Kujenga's arms, holding him steady. The other hunkered down to the ground, using his whole body, straddling Kujenga's left leg, pressing his foot flat to the ground. The next moment, Hackett walked out of the barn, a long, heavy, sledgehammer in his hand. It was like the sledgehammer's they used to drive railroad spikes, a silver metal head at the end of a long piece of wood.

Entering the clearing, Hackett spit into both his hands before taking up the sledgehammer, he raised it high over his head.

Realizing what was about to happen, Kujenga began struggling. Being bigger, far stronger than the men holding him, he tossed them off like most folks swat sketters. Four more of Gethen's men rush forward to help. It took a few minutes for them to get him under control, held in position.

Not knowing how long they could hold Kujenga, Hackett acted fast. He raised the hammer, bringing it down hard on Kujenga's left foot.

There was a thunderous thud, followed by Kujenga screaming, breaking free from the men, falling to the ground.

Hackett stood over Kujenga.

"That'll teach ya." He turned, smiling to Gethen standing on the porch. "Take him into the barn. See he's chained up real good," was his order to his men.

When the hammer came down, every one of us cringed, shouting out our horror. As they carried Kujenga to the barn, no one said a word. No tears were shed for him, except by me, and surprisingly, my mother.

When I woke the next morning, everyone in my family was gone. My mother felt it best I get rest, not returning to work until I was strong enough. She could handle the main house kitchen by herself till then.

A knock at the front door startled me. I knew my family was working. I got up from bed with the blanket wrapped around me. Opening the door just enough to lookout, I was confronted with the face of the last person I expected to see. It was Treven Gilley dressed in his leather outfit, holding his horsehide hat in his hand.

"Yes?" I asked shyly.

"Miss Audean, I'd like a moment of your time. There's something I need to tell you."

"I don't think we have anything to talk about," I said, clearly sounding short with him.

"Please, I know you're angry with me. You have a good right to be. But it's not what you think. I have some good news for you."

"Go ahead; I'm listening."

"I'd rather come in and speak in private. What I have to say is for your ears only."

"Wait one minute while I put on some clothes."

I closed the door, returning to my room. As I dressed, I figured what did I have to lose in listening to him. I hid one of my mother's knives in my apron. If he tried anything, I'd kill him. An idea that went through my mind the moment I saw him at our front door.

"Come in," I said, holding the door open.

He walked in, closing the door behind him. We stood in the center of the room, a few feet from each other. I kept my hand in my pocket with a firm grip on the kitchen knife.

"So, what is it ya wanna tell me that's so important?"

"I know you're close with Kujenga. You probably don't trust me. I understand."

"Kujenga... then ya know his name, do ya?"

"Yes, he told it to me when I spoke with him."

This amazed me, leaving me confused.

Gilley continued, "I'm sorry about what they did to him. It wasn't part of the plan."

"Plan... what plan?"

"Who do you think helped him to escape, in the first place? I was the one who cut his chains, setting him free."

Now, I was completely baffled.

"I make my living hunting down runaway slaves. I can't just wait around for slaves to run off. Sometimes, I have to make it happen. I heard about Kujenga. I know his kind. I knew if he were to escape, they wouldn't catch him. I snuck into the barn and made a deal with him. If I helped him escape, he would allow me to catch him."

"Why would he do that?" I asked.

"The deal is if he did this, I'd help him to escape a second time, this time with you."

"But that's not how it turned out," I said.

"No, you came into the picture. Instead, he gave himself up for your sake. Still, I got my money. I plan to keep my promise to him."

"But his foot, they broke his foot," I insisted.

"That's why I'll have to wait till he heals. It may take months, but I'll be back. Don't worry. He's no ordinary man, in his world he was a great warrior. He'll surely limp for the rest of his life, nevertheless, it will never stop him."

It all seemed so mindboggling to me. Still, there was no reason for me not to believe him. He had nothing to gain by telling me his story. Then, another thought came into my head.

"Ya can talk with him?" I asked.

"Yes," Gilley said, smiling. "I was raised in Africa. Kujenga speaks a form of Swahili like mine. I can understand most of it."

"Tell me what he said."

"Well, he's from a small tribe in South Africa. His grandfather was the chief of the village. His father died when he was a baby. He was raised by his mother, under the wings of his grandparents. His life was no different from any other boy in the village. From an early age, they taught him to hunt and to fight. He knows how to do both well, which is why they couldn't track him down. I could never track him down either. If not for our agreement, I never would stand a chance of finding him. Then, when you were hurt, he brought you back. It made it all the easier. Like I said, I'm a man of my word. I'll be back in a few months, when he's healed. I'll make good on our deal."

"Did he say anything else…about me?" I asked, shyly.

His smile grew larger.

"Girl, you've got nothing to worry about. There's no question about it. That man loves you. He's a big man, with a big love for you."

He stepped to the door, opened it, beginning to walk out.

"I'll see you in a few months."

I called to him, "Mr. Gilley?"

"Call me Treven."

"Treven…thank ya."

Fifteen

You Win

Weeks later, I still wasn't feeling well, my strength was still waning; nevertheless, they made me return to work. Only, it wasn't in the kitchen. I'm sure Gethen thought of it as my punishment. My new job was in the fields with the others, picking cotton.

This put more workload on my mother. Running the kitchen was difficult enough with two people. Now, alone, Mama worked twice as hard. It would seem the mother suffered for the sins of the daughter.

As for my father, continuing to work in the fields, he received orders he no longer needed to take meals to Kujenga during the day, only his meal in the evening. There was a reason for this. The mysterious reason made clear in time.

It was early in the morning. The sun was still low on the horizon. The best time of the day, the air still cool from the night, the heat of the day was hours away. There was the sound of chains rattling. We looked up from our work to see two overseers guiding Kujenga toward us.

Like me, he still wasn't fully healed. You could see it in his eyes. He limped as he walked. A wave of pain washed over his face whenever he brought his bad foot down. They'd shackled his feet, forcing him to take small steps. His hands were in front of him, connected by a chain with many links, giving him enough play to use his hands for work.

It took a few minutes of pantomime for Hackett to get his point across. Kujenga was to pick cotton, along with the rest of us. Again, surely, this was Gethen's way of punishing Kujenga. If he wouldn't play along with Gethen's game, he would suffer like the rest of us.

Our eyes met. This brought us both comfort. However, when I tried to get close to him, one of the overseers made sure I kept my distance. Obviously, Gethen warned them to keep us apart.

It was a long day of hard work in the heat, except it was far worse for Kujenga. Clearly, he was in pain, trying all-day to keep his weight off his swollen foot, bound in heavy chains only made matters worse.

As well, the overseers would often take a whip to his back or hit him with the butt of their rifle. There seemed to be no particular reason for this punishment other than the shear enjoyment of inflicting pain on someone who couldn't fight back. I'm sure, Gethen ordered this. Still, it was clear how much pleasure they got from dishing out hurt on someone so helpless. It was the powerful preying on the powerless. It was plain to see by his size and strength, if Kujenga were allowed two minutes with any of them; he would crush them with his bare hands like a walnut.

Pain, torture, made for a long hard day, though nothing compared to the hurt brought on by the way the other slaves treated Kujenga. No one approached him. I would have, if they let me. No one spoke to him. They ignored him, some to the point of refusing to as much as look at him.

Some, understandably, knew he'd fallen out of Gethen's favor. Not wanting any trouble, they wanted nothing to do with him.

It was those who refused to accept him that upset me, hurting him the most. They were slaves. Now, *they* had someone they could look down on. It was a new experience for some, and they reveled in it.

"He may look like one of us, but he ain't," said an old woman, as we sat on the ground, eating our midday meal. Kujenga ate alone. His chains clanking as he brought the food to his mouth. "Just look at him. He's a savage, a creation of Satan."

"Satan can't create anything," someone argued.

"Then he's Satan's child. I wish he never come here." The old woman put down her plate, turned, looking me square in the eye. "Child, ya don't know how lucky ya be that ya lost that baby. It be a demon, for sure."

I was beside myself with anger. I wanted so much to throw my plate of food in her face. Hundreds of cruel things to say to her flooded my mind. I looked at my father sitting on the ground across from me. I saw the sympathy in his eyes. In the end, I thought it best for all to not say a word. I rose, walked a few yards away, sat back down, finishing my meal, alone.

The rest of the day was the same for Kujenga. He worked alone in silence. Every so often, one of the overseers trashed him for no reason. At the end of the day, they took Kujenga back to the barn where they chained him to the post for the night. As originally arranged, my father delivered his evening meal. Papa never complained about this duty though by his facial expression you could tell he wasn't pleased. As always, no matter how I begged, he never told me how Kujenga was alone in that barn. So, after a time, I quit asking him.

Weeks passed, nothing changed for Kujenga. If anything, it got worse. The treatment he received was inhumane, and it showed in Kujenga's appearance, in the way his shoulders slummed in defeat. The good thing was that his foot was healing, although, as Treven Gilley pointed out, Kujenga would limp for the rest of his life.

One particular day, while working in the fields, I looked over to Kujenga picking cotton a few yards away. The moment our eyes met, an overseer bashed him in the back of the head with the butt of his rifle. Kujenga went to his knees. I was so angered, feeling so helpless. Yet, it was at that moment the truth came to me.

All along I thought, like all the others. I thought that Gethen turned Kujenga's life to the worst it could be because he wouldn't mate with any other slave girl other than me. Then it dawned on me, this treatment wasn't a punishment, nor was it to persuade Kujenga to do Gethen's bidding. It had all been done for me. Gethen knew the connection between Kujenga and I was strong. If I watched Kujenga suffer, hard and long enough, I would give into Gethen's plans, becoming his ally.

Putting down my gathering sack, I walked over to Hackett.

"What'd ya want, girl?"

"I want to get a message to the Massa. I need to talk to him."

"Ya do, do ya? Would that be over a cup-a-tea at his place or yours?"

"Just tell him that I give up. He won. I'll do whatever he says."

"Oh, and what would that be?"

"Just tell him, he'll know."

It would seem Hackett knew as well. He immediately left for the main house.

During our meal at midday, as I sat on the ground next to my father, Hackett returned. He stood over us, looking down, smiling.

"Come with me, girl."

My father shot a questioning look to me.

"What's this all about?"

"It's all right, Papa, I know what I'm doin'."

"I pray to God ya do."

I stood up, following Hackett to the main house.

****

Entering the library, Hackett guided me to stand in the center of the room.

"Don't touch anything," he warned as he left, closing the door behind him.

I waited nervously, eyeing the fineness of the room. Full shelves of books covered every wall. In those days, they looked down on white folks who taught blacks to read. In some parts of the country, it was illegal. At that time in my life, I couldn't read or write a single word. I wouldn't even have recognized my own name in writing. Strangely enough, though I had much more important things on my mind at the time, it was at that moment that I swore someday I would learn to read and write.

Just then, the library door opened, in walked Gethen. Without so much as looking at me, he walked past, standing behind his desk.

"Hackett tells me you have something to say. Go ahead, I'm listening."

I waited a moment before replying, thinking of the best way to say it. I wanted to get my point across, yet, I didn't want to get on Gethen's bad side.

"I understand your position with Kujenga, sir."

"Kujenga…who is this Kujenga?"

I wanted to erupt; still, I kept my calm. Perhaps, he never learned Kujenga's name, or he was playing with me, wanting to see me dance.

"Kujenga…the slave ya keeps in the barn."

"Oh, you mean the savage. What about him?"

"I know ya want him to do some fathering. I nearly had his baby."

"Yes, I know. It's a shame you lost it."

He said the word *Shame* in a way it was clear he didn't mean it as sympathy for me or the child, but for time and money lost, his time, his money.

Staring down at my shoes, I shyly continued, "I'd be willin' to have his baby, again, if only…"

"If only I'd let you return to work in the kitchen alongside your mother," he interrupted. "Working in the field seems to have brought you to your senses."

"No, sir, that's not what I been thinkin'. I been seein' the way they treat him. If only they would stop beatin' on him."

"Oh, so now you're telling me how to run my plantation?"

"No, sir, that's not what I was thinkin'. I just figured a man can't do no fathering if he's in misery."

Gethen let out a long hard laugh. "It seems, Missy, you don't know men very well. But I like your spunk. I'll tell you what. I'll have the men lighten up on him. Only, you must keep your end of the bargain. I'll allow your visiting this savage every night in the barn. Just understand, if you are not with child within three months, there will be hell to pay, both for you and this…savage."

"Yes, sir, I understand."

"You may leave, now," he announced. "Oh, another thing," he said before I left. I turned to face him. "You're allowed to work in the kitchen with your mother, again. I'll have the men lighten up on this savage, but he'll continue to work in the fields. Also, your father will continue to bring him his evening meals"

"Yes, sir," I said, opening the library door.

"One last thing," he said as I was leaving. "Don't ever mention wanting to marry this beast. It will never happen. And get it into that tiny skull of yours that once you have this baby, you're not going to be his one and only. There will be other women and other children."

"Yes, sir…."

Sixteen

The Savage's Woman

Oh, how my mother cried when she learned of my plans. She could hardly speak. My father refused to say a word to me. But what could they do? To go against the Massa's wishes was asking for more trouble.

My sister, Deidra, felt confused. Late at night, alone, she would ask me a million questions. Finally, yielding to the belief that true love triumphs over all, she gave me her blessing, though both of us knew any relationship between Kujenga and I was doomed from the start. We never spoke about such things, again. She wouldn't, not wanting to upset me, and I for wanting to not even think about it.

As for my brother, Lucius, he paid it no mind. He was still at the age when all matters concerning adults made no sense to him. Such foolishness needed to be ignored at all cost. Little did he know a time would come when matters of the heart and soul become foremost.

After the dust settled, my mother sat me down at the table in the main house kitchen for a mother-daughter heart-to-heart.

"Ya are my first child. I love ya more than ya ever know. I want ya to be happy, safe, a good woman. This boy, he ain't like none of us. His ways ain't our ways. There are so many nice boys around. Why ya wanna be with this...."

I knew the word Mama wanted to say. For the sake of not burning the bridge between us, she held back.

"Mama, I know ya love me. I know ya worry. This is the one for me." A question came to mind, "How did ya know Papa was the one?"

She chuckled, "I don't think I ever thought about it. I just knew.'

"That's how I feel about Kujenga."

She looked at me funny.

"Kujenga...that's his name, Mama, won't ya at least call him by his name?"

She rose from her chair, walking to the stove. She looked out the window as she spoke. "I can't," she replied, sadly. "Perhaps, someday...only...not today." She turned, looking to me. "Be careful, Audean. Please, be careful."

"I will, Mama."

||*|*|*|*

79

On the first night that I was to spend in the barn with Kujenga, everyone in my family kept to themselves. No one said a word, especially to me. When I stepped out on our small porch, I found my father sitting in his rocking chair. He'd been drinking, a rare thing for my father to do. It was understandable, under the circumstance, knowing how he felt.

As I walked passed him, I feared he might say something to me, although, I found his icy silence far worse. When I stepped off the porch, he called to me, startling me. His voice, soft and low, muddled from the whiskey.

"Where ya goin', girl?" he asked, knowing the answer, but asking it all the same for his own reasons.

"I'm goin' out, Papa," was my poor reply. I felt too ashamed to put it into words.

He pushed further, "Out where?"

There was no call to not say the truth. He would not let go until he heard it from my lips.

"I'm goin' to the barn, Papa."

"The barn...what'cha gonna do in the barn?"

There was no way I would escape it. I took in a deep breath, letting out the truth. "I'm gonna spend the night with Kujenga."

"Kujenga...ya mean that savage."

I had no response to that.

Papa took another sip of whiskey for courage.

"So, tell me, girl. When did ya and this savage get married? I don't remember a weddin'."

"We're not married, Papa." I whispered, staring at the ground, a lump in my throat.

"What did ya say? Speak up, girl, I can't hear ya."

"I said, 'We ain't married, Papa'."

"That's what I thought ya said." He stared at me through tearful eyes. "Is that what we taught ya? Is that how we raised ya?"

"Ya don't understand, Papa."

"Damn straight, I don't understand!"

"I'm sorry, Papa. It's the only way."

"It's the only way that ya can see from where ya standin', but it ain't the only way."

I couldn't take much more. I started to back away from the porch, into the darkness. Papa stood up, staggered to the edge of the porch, taking hold of one of the post for support.

"If he harms one hair on your head, I'll kill him. I swear to God, I'll kill him."

I was deep in darkness. I turned, walking away.

"Audean, I love ya," he shouted out.

"I love ya, too, Papa," I called back over my shoulder.

****

The barn door creaked, as I slowly opened it. I found Kujenga standing, wearing a worried look, which disappeared as soon as he saw me. His face lit up.

"Audean!" he shouted, his arms outstretched. He would have run to me, if not for the chain around his neck holding him in place.

I ran to him, falling into his arms. He encircled me in his embrace. I forgot what it felt like to feel safe. My tears ran down my cheeks, wetting his chest. He eased up, holding my face in his hands.

"Love, Audean," he whispered, kissing the tears from off my face. This only made me cry the more.

Our lips met. We kissed deep and hard. His strong arms lifted me up, gently placing me down. We lay on our sides, holding on to each other for dear life. No words were needed between us. Each touch sang of love, every kiss was a sonnet.

His mouth moved along my neck and throat, moving slowly down. I wrapped my arms around his neck, pulling him closer, holding him in place, not wanting him to ever stop.

Like the shadow of a cloud moving over the meadow, he coved his body over mine. Pressing his full weight down on me, I took hold of the muscles in his back. I closed my eyes. I was finally home, for he *was* my home.

****

Weeks went by. They were weeks of mixed feelings. For I spent most nights in the arms of my beloved, our love growing like the cotton in the fields he worked each day, with new blossoms each morning. This was the good part.

The bad, the sad and unhappy part was in the way our entire world saw us and how they treated us.

My family remained cold to me. Even working full days with my mother in the main house kitchen, few words were spoken. My father found excuses to avoid me, steering clear of any possible confrontation. All words spoke to me by my parents were commands, nothing more, never asking, avoiding the subject on all our minds at all costs. The cost being the love we once shared as a family.

But the hardest, cruelest moments were with our fellow slaves. Kujenga worked the fields, as he'd done before, only now, thankfully, he no longer received abuse from the overseers, that is. As for the others, the other workers, slaves like him; they ignored him, avoiding him like the plague. No one spoke to him, interacted with him, and in many cases ignored him to the point of refusing to as much as look in his direction. If by accident he did come in contact with any one of them, he received the cold shoulder, the icy stare, and often spit on.

As for me, if he was the savage that they shunned, then I was the savage's woman, lowest of the low, and hated as much, if not more, than he. I was one of them. I should know better, acting differently, in line with their beliefs. I was a traitor, no longer one of them, deserving nothing less than banishment, or worse, if it were up to some.

No one spoke to me, unless it was necessary, and that was only to a point with no civility. Folks looked the other way when I passed by. If a pair of eyes met mine, they were filled with hatred, shooting daggers at me. As discouraging as this was, it didn't sway me from my feelings for Kujenga. If anything, it drew me closer to him. They were no longer my world, he was.

****

I was spending at least four nights each week in the barn with Kujenga. It all became second nature to us both. It was as close to setting up house together as the powers that be would allow. Each day was long and torturous, putting my head down, working, waiting for it to end. Being with Kujenga became my only joy. The entire day felt as if I were holding my breath. Only at night, in Kujenga's arms, was I able to breathe. My entire world was in that barn. The outside world was miles away. Only in the night, in his arms, did I come alive to live.

There was a chill in the night. We lay close, his arm around me. My eyes closed, though we didn't sleep, just resting in the afterglow. He opened his eyes when I took his hand, placing it on my flat belly. I moved his hand in a circle.

"Baby," I said softly. "I'm gonna have a baby."

Kujenga sat up, keeping his hand on my belly. A smile appeared on his face, growing larger as he spoke, his eyes wide.

"Mtoto?" he whispered rubbing his hand gently over me. "Mtoto?" he asked, again.

Somehow, I understood what he was saying.

"Yes, Mtoto…Mtoto," I whispered back, smiling, lovingly looking into his eyes.

"Mtoto wa kike? Mtoto wa kiume?" he asked, looking concerned.

I thought it over. I now understood Mtoto meant baby. But what did *wa kike* and *wa kiume* mean? Then it dawned on me.

"A boy or a girl, ya want to know if it's a boy or a girl. I don't know. There's no way I can," I laughed.

Kujenga laughed along with me. Guiding me to lie flat, he hovered his head inches above my belly.

"Mtoto," he said, sounding very serious. Then he leaned down, kissing my belly. "Mtoto," he said, again.

He brought his head up. We kissed.

"Love Audean," he whispered in my ear.

"Love Kujenga," I said softly.

****

"I told you once before, there are no secrets on my plantation. Gossip moves over it like wildfire."

There I was again standing in the main house library before Furcas Gethen. He sat behind his large desk. There were empty chairs, but he never offered me a seat. So, I stood, listening.

"I saw Hackett this morning. He told me you might have something to tell me."

I had only told my mother about being with child. I didn't say anything to her about not telling anyone. Perhaps, I should have. Now, the entire plantation knew about my circumstance, including the Massa.

I'd long since lost my shyness about such matters, confronting him boldly. "Yes, I am carrying Kujenga's child."

Gethen laughed, "Oh, that's right. You like to call him by his name," he said, mocking me. "That's good," he continued. "Now, he'll finally earn his keep." Gethen sat back, eyeing me from head to toe. "I don't want what happened the last time to happen. I don't want this baby to be lost. I want you to move into the main house with us, so we can keep an eye on you, keep you healthy, and make sure you have this baby."

I stood speechless, looking through him, staring blankly.

"You can still work in the kitchen with your mother; just don't do any heavy lifting. We have a small room upstairs, you can move in tonight. That reminds me, no more nightly visits to the barn, in fact, no more visits of any kind."

"I don't understand," I spoke up. "I thought this is what ya wanted?"

"It is, and I'm going to make sure you have the child, which is why you will be staying in my house."

"Please, sir, let me continue being with Kujenga. I promise, once I have this child, I'll have another and then another. I'll just keep havin' babies, I promise."

"And you will...keep having babies, that is, but you won't be the only one. He's going to father many children with many girls. And this time it will be different. They'll be no hunger strikes and no escapes. I had it all wrong. When he wouldn't do what I demanded, I tried to punish him. I had it all wrong. This time, if he doesn't do what I want, it will be you who I'll punish." Gethen laughed.

Seventeen

What Happened to Treven Gilley

Treven Gilley had a plan. It was to get rich, buy a ranch in South America, living the rest of his life in peace. Being a free black man allowed him to move freely, offering more potential to achieve his dream than other black folks who were slaves, their potential being nil.

The fly in the ointment was this. Treven Gilley had no skills to carry out his plan. Still, he was blessed with a quick and inventive mind, his only armor and weapon in his arsenal.

His scheme was this. Create the façade he was an expert African tracker, specializing in tracking down runaway slaves. Of course, there was no such animal. It was all a lie, a creation of his imagination. Still, the people bought it.

The illusion was formed by exotic clothes, eccentric behavior, always relying on his charm, quick wit, and vivid imagination.

As for him being a crackerjack tracker, Treven Gilley couldn't find a cowbell if it was tied around his neck. All that he needed was to give the impression that he could. He did this with great finesse.

The plot was this. He secretly meets with a plantation slave who wanted to desperately run away. These are usually single, young men. With his connection to the Underground Railroad, he could assure them a good chance of running to freedom. There was only one catch. The slave agreed to be set free and brought to a hiding place provided by Treven, one only he knew about. Treven would then make a deal with the plantation owner to track down and return the runaway slave for a fee. The agreement between Treven and the slave was that after he captured and returned the slave, claiming his reward, Treven would return to free the slave, again. He would share ten percent of the reward with the slave, and then hand him over to the Underground Railroad. It seemed a foolproof plan, but only a fool thinks in those terms. Treven's plan succeeded for many years, until one unexpected day. Didn't Shakespeare mention something about the plans of mice and men?

****

Curtis Baker was a sassy young man with a bad habit of talking back to the overseers of the Collins Plantation. Most black slaves on a cotton plantation knew their place in the world, but not Curtis. He never accepted his lot in life.

If an overseer ordered him to move faster, he moved slower. If told to go left, he went right. Disobedience came at a high cost, usually a dozen lashes. Curtis' back looked like an embroidered doily made of black lace. Yet, he never was dismayed.

As severe as going under the lash was, there were worse punishments for worse crimes then sassing back. To strike an overseer meant death, usually by hanging. Talking back to an overseer meant time in the *Box*. The Box was a simple contraption. An upright, coffin shaped metal box with just enough room to stand in, and impossible to do anything but stand. The temperature within the box was always ten to twenty degrees hotter in the daytime and at least ten degrees colder during the night. A slave could expect a stay in the box for an infraction for up to three days, being given no food and little water. Standing up three days in the Box brought a person within inches of death. No one ever survived more than six days. Curtis' sassy mouth landed him in the Box for a seven-day stint. It was on the night of the third day that Curtis Baker met Treven Gilley.

Three days of standing up in the Box took its toll on Curtis. He ached from head to toe. His throat was parched, his tongue was swollen. No food for three days allowed him to put his finger between his now protruding ribs. He was shaking as if he had a fever. The sweat that drenched his body all-day long, now in the deep of night, chilled him to the bone.

From the lack of sound, he sensed it was the middle of the night. He was just about to mercifully fall asleep when a tap on the side of the metal Box startled him.

"You still alive?" a voice seeped through the steel casing.

Curtis didn't answer for fear it might be one of the overseers checking on him. Or, perhaps, he was dreaming, or worse, hallucinating. It was a cold fact that folks who stayed long periods in the Box would begin to see visions and hear voices. Then again, perhaps this was the voice of Death himself coming to check on him, ready to take him to the Promised Land. Maybe, he was dead, already. Whatever the reason, Curtis hesitated to answer.

"Are you still alive?" the voice repeated. A moment passed. "If you don't answer me, I assume you're dead. If you're dead then there's no reason to open this box and let you out."

Whoever the voice belonged to, Curtis couldn't take the chance of turning down such an offer.

"Yes, I'm alive."

"Good! Now, listen carefully. I have a proposition for you."

Curtis began to think he *was* hallucinating.

"I'll let you out and bring you to someone I know with the Underground Railroad. They will take you to a northern state where you will be a free man. I'll do this for you, only I need you to do something for me, first."

"What's that?" Curtis asked, sounding skeptical.

"I will set you free, and then bring you to a place where you'll be safe. You can hide out there for about a week. After that time, I'll bring you back here so I can claim a finder's reward. About a week later, I'll come back to free you, all over again, and bring you to the Underground Railroad. I'll even give you a hundred dollars to help start you on your new life."

Now, Curtis knew he was hallucinating. Still, he had questions.

"How do I know y'all do what ya says y'all gonna do?" Curtis asked.

"You don't. However, if you don't agree to my terms, I'll leave you where you are. I would suspect you'll be dead in a day or two. With that in mind, what have you got to lose?"

Curtis didn't have to think long. Be it the voice of death or a voice in his delusional mind, Curtis saw no other way than to consent.

"I agree to your terms," Curtis announced.

The latch on the Box clicked. The door swung open. The cold night air hit Curtis like a hammer to his head. He fell, unconscious, into someone's arms.

****

Curtis woke to find he was lying on a bed, in a one-room cabin. There was only one window. The daylight felt good. There was a table and two chairs in the center of the room. To one side there was a miniature Franklin stove filling the cabin with warmth. He was alone.

The door swung open. In walked a man carrying an armful of firewood. He walked over to stove, placing the logs on the floor. Curtis stared at the man for he was an eyeful. Dressed completely in leather, beads around his neck, a horsehide hat, he was a sight.

"Oh, you're awake," said the man, turning around to him.

Curtis tried to sit up in the bed, only he was too weak. He fell down onto his back.

"Don't try to get up. It'll take a few days for you to get your strength back. My name is Treven Gilley, and you are...?"

"Curtis Baker."

"Well, Curtis, I do hope you remember the bargain we agreed to last night."

"Where are we?" Curtis asked.

"Someplace safe, no one will find you here."

"What color are ya?" Curtis asked bluntly.

Treven laughed. "Does it matter? But if you must know, my father was white and my mother was black."

"So, what does that make you?" Curtis asked.

"Me." was Treven's answer.

Treven took a coffeepot off the stove, pouring them both a cup.

"Here, drink this, it'll warm you up."

With great effort, Curtis propped up on his elbow, taking the cup. He spoke between sips.

"So, what do we do next?" Curtis asked.

"*We* don't do anything," Treven replied. "You stay here, safe and sound, while I go back to the plantation and arrange a fee for your capture." Treven took the pot of coffee, placing it on the table. "I suggest you stay in bed for a day or so until you get your strength back. At the foot of the bed there's a pitcher of water. When you feel up to it, there's a creek a few yards west of here. Next to the pitcher is a week's worth of food. When that runs out, you're on your own. But you should be up and about by then. Oh, and there's a chamber pot under the bed."

"You'll be gone more than a week?" Curtis asked.

"Probably, I gotta make it look good. You know, scowl the countryside looking for you."

Treven started for the door.

Curtis had a worried look in his eyes.

"Ya really gonna bring me in, and then come back to free me, all over again?"

"I said I would. I don't make promises I can't keep. Treven Gilley is a man of his word. I'll see you in a few weeks."

He walked out. Curtis rested back down onto the bed, the cup of warm coffee on his chest. He listened to the sound of Treven's horse galloping away.

****

Treven was right. After two days, Curtis felt strong enough to move about the cabin. The next day he was well enough to venture outside, which was good because the water pitcher was empty. He had no problem finding the stream. He could hear the rushing water, as soon as he stepped out of the cabin.

What little food Treven left him, Curtis ate sparingly, first eating the food that would perish quickest. A week later, the food was gone. Curtis went out gathering. He lived on nuts, roots, berries, and frogs that he caught at the creek.

Curtis woke one morning to the sound of horse's hooves off in the distance coming closer. His first instinct was to run and hide, except, where to? He got out of bed, to the front door, and stood in the doorway. Thankfully, it was Treven. He was alone.

"Well, Curtis, today's the day. You're going back."

Curtis tried to prepare for this day, only now that it was here; fear ran through him.

"What if they punish me? What if they hang me?"

"And waste good money. No, you're worth more to them alive. But it wouldn't surprise me if they gave you a good lashing or they stuck you back in the Box for a few days. You need to be prepared."

Silently, Curtis closed the door to the cabin, walking over to Treven and his horse. Treven reached down, hoisting Curtis up onto the horse, sitting in the rear.

"It's not far," Treven said. "You can ride with me most of the way, but when we get in sight of the plantation, you're going to have to get down and walk."

When they came over the hill, looking down at the Collins Plantation, Treven got Curtis down off the horse. He tied Curtis' hands in front of him, forcing him to walk.

Their reception when they came to the front of the main house was a cold one. Other slaves looked on with sad eyes. Treven handed Curtis over to the overseers. They handed him his money. Without a word, Treven rode away and out of sight. As predicted, Curtis was immediately place in the Box.

****

"Are you awake?" Treven whispered at the Box.

"Treven, is that y'all?" Curtis replied.

"Listen, Curtis, we've got a problem. They put a lock on the latch. I'm going to have to shoot it off. I need you to stand back."

"How the hell am I gonna stand back in this thing?" Curtis answered.

It was a strange request, still, Treven continued, as if nothing was wrong.

"Curtis…when I shoot the lock off, it's going to wake everybody. You're going to need to move fast. We need to get on my horse and fly out of here, before they know what's happened. You ready?"

"Yeah, I'm ready."

Treven took his pistol from his holster, placing the muzzle against the lock. He pulled the gun hammer back, took a deep breath, pulling the trigger. The gunshot shattered the quiet of the night, the ricochet echoed numerous times. The lock was damaged, but still intact.

"It's still locked. I've got to try, again," Treven declared.

"Please, hurry," Curtis pleaded.

Treven fired, again. This time the lock burst into pieces. The latch was hot to the touch, burning Treven's fingers as he lifted it.

As soon as the door opened, Curtis jumped out of the Box. They mounted Treven's horse, galloping away. They heard shouting behind them, getting farther off in the distance as they raced into the night.

****

They rode for two days, only stopping momentarily so the horse could rest. Treven's stamina was something to admire. He never let up, putting as many miles between their pursuers and them. Curtis found it difficult to stay awake. More than once, he fell asleep, loosening his grip, falling from the horse onto the ground. Treven shook him awake, picked him up, put him back on the horse, and continued.

On the morning of the third day, they stopped in a clearing.

"We're to meet her here," Treven said, taking the saddle off his horse, giving the poor beast a well-earned rest.

"Her...?" Curtis asked, taken aback.

"Why, you got a problem with that?" Treven said.

"No...no problem, I'm just surprised."

They lay in the grass, resting, waiting.

Two hours later they heard a rustle in the high grass. Curtis sat up to see an old black woman leading a donkey coming toward them. She was petite. Her strides were short, but she moved quickly. She was dressed in the typical house slave manner, full petticoat and apron, her head covered with a red and white scarf. She looked ancient. There was no way of guessing how old she was. The lines in her face and on her hands suggested many years.

Treven jumped to his feet to greet her. Curtis rose to his feet, as well.

"Minty, it's good to see you," Treven called out. "How have you been?"

"Fair to Midland," the old woman responded. Stopping, she looked Curtis up and down. "Is this the new boy ya told me about? He ain't much to look at."

"Hey, wait a minute," Curtis objected. He looked to Treven. "I got half the countryside lookin' for me. If they catch me this time, they'll kill me, for sure. And ya hand me over to this old lady!"

"Hey, watch your mouth," Treven demanded. "Show a little respect. Minty, here's been working the Underground Railroad since you were a nipper."

Minty stepped forward, looking up, eye to eye with Curtis.

"Listen, child, ya know what the Underground Railroad is?"

Curtis shrugged his shoulders.

"It's a long line of safe houses runnin' from here to up north. Since ya don't know the way and I does, it'd best be ya shut that rattletrap of yours and do what I says or I'll shut it for ya."

Treven bent over laughing at how well Minty put Curtis in his place.

"Now, lift me up onto this beast, and let's move it," Minty ordered.

Both Treven and Curtis lifted Minty onto the donkey. Treven reached in his pocket, taking out two gold coins. He handed one to Curtis.

"Here you go, Curtis, this is your cut of the reward money that I promised you."

Curtis looked at the coin in his hand and then at Treven.

"Treven, I don't know how I could ever thank ya," Curtis' voice broke slightly.

"Now, don't get all mushy on me. You just do whatever Minty tells you."

Treven walked to Minty, placed the second coin in her hand, bent over and kissed her cheek.

"Here you go, Minty, a little something for the cause."

Curtis took the reins of the beast, turned it around, and started to guide it north with Minty atop.

"Ya'll stay outta trouble, ya hear?" Minty called back over her shoulder to Treven.

Curtis looked back one last time.

"God bless ya, Treven," Curtis said.

"Yeah...sure...right," Treven said nervously, for such talk made him that way, as he watched them walk off, disappearing into the northern forest.

Eighteen

The Hanging of Treven Gilley

"Who the hell are you?" asked the guard at the door.

"I've come to see the prisoner," the old woman replied.

"Well, you can see him in an hour when we hang him."

"I've come to see the prisoner. I'm his mother."

"That's just too bad," the guard replied, closing the door in her face.

The next moment the door opens, again. There's another guard with the first guard is standing behind him.

"For God sake, Pete, let the woman see her son one last time before it's too late."

He allowed her in, guiding her through the office to another door leading to the backroom where there are jail cells. He walked her past two empty cells to the last one.

"You got five minutes," he told her as he walked away, leaving the room.

Treven was lying stretched out on his cot. When he saw her, he jumped to his feet, rushed to the door of the cell, gripping the bars.

His voice was shaky, "Minty!"

They remained silent for a moment, staring at each other.

He smiled at her, "Thanks for coming,"

"Ya really did it this time," Minty said.

"Yeah, it looks that way."

"Ya need anything?"

"A hacksaw and a shotgun," he laughed.

Minty wasn't laughing.

"There is one thing you can do for me."

Minty didn't answer. She waited for the request.

"There's a slave at the old Gethen place. You know it?"

She nodded.

"Well, I promised this here slave I'd come back, free him, and get him to you. Only, it looks like I won't be able to."

"And ya want me to go get him," Minty added.

"If you would, I'd appreciate it. Think of it as a dying man's last request." Again, he found humor in this, as Minty found none. "There is one problem" he continued. "They got him chained up in the barn, and he don't speak a lick of English."

"That's never stopped me, before," she assured him.

"Time's up!" said the guard, bursting into the room.

"You gonna stay for the festivities?" Treven asked, wearing a half-smile.

She nodded, reaching out, placing her hand on his hand for a moment.

"Let's go," the guard demanded.

The guard guided her out of the room, Treven returned to his cot.

****

"Good size crowd. I must be famous," Treven shouted over the dim of the crowd to the guards guiding him to the scaffold. He tried to put up a brave front, but while climbing the steps up to the platform, his knees went weak. They helped him up the last few steps.

He smiled into the face of the hangman, "Enjoy your work, do you?"

There was no response.

The two guards guided the hand-bound Treven to stand on the hatch. They tied his feet together at his ankles, placing the noose around his neck.

He looked around, nervously, hoping to see Minty. He didn't see her. Still, he felt her presence. A small old woman like Minty would easily be lost in a crowd.

"Don't I get to say any last words?" he asked the guards.

They ignored him. The hangman walked over to the edge of the scaffold, taking hold of the lever.

Treven looked out at the crowd.

"I've never seen so many pasty-face sons-a-bitches in all my life," he shouted, just as the hangman pulled the lever.

His body flew downward, the rope went tight, and he bounced a few times, and then went motionless. The crowd cheered.

Chapter Nineteen

Like You Want To Be Treated

It was the loneliest time in my life. I worked all-day in the kitchen with my mother, barely saying two words to each other. At the end of the day when I would normally go to the slave's quarters to friends and family, instead I would go up to my room in the main house, spending the night alone. Although perhaps it was best, seeing how I was on the outs with both friends and family.

I don't know if it was a coincidence or Gethen did it on purpose to make my life miserable, but the only window in my room looked directly at the front of the barn. Knowing Kujenga was only a few feet away, a few feet I wasn't allowed to cross was torture for me.

I never retired to my room early enough to see Kujenga return from working in the fields. He was already chained up in the barn by then. However, I did get to see my father delivering Kujenga's meals every night. He would stay in the barn for a long time, coming out nearly an hour later with the empty plate, which he brought back to the kitchen. I could only believe my father waited for Kujenga to finish his meal, watching him eat every bite.

I'd never been so alone in my life. I often went to bed early to escape the long hours. Many were the nights I cried myself to sleep. I thought I hadn't a friend in the world. That is until one night there was a surprising knock on my bedroom door.

"Yes, who is it?" I whispered to the closed door.

Whoever it was ignored my need for privacy. Thankfully, I had not yet removed my clothes. The door slowly opened. It was Jason and Jenny, Furcas Gethen's two young children. They were already wearing their nightgowns. Without my invitation, they entered.

Both were younger than I by only a couple of years, still childlike. They were both handsome offspring, inheriting their mother's good looks with chestnut hair and violet eyes. Jason, being the oldest, was slightly taller by two to three inches.

Over the years, they saw me working in the kitchen, though saying very little to one another. Mostly, they ignored me as if I were invisible, only now, they stared at me with great fascination.

"Father says we're not to talk to you or even come near you," Jenny said in a defiant tone.

"He says you're going to have a baby," Jason added. "Is that true?"

"Yes, it is," I responded.

"He says you're having the savage's baby."

I don't know what made me say it. Perhaps, I didn't feel they were a threat. Still, it was a foolish thing to say. "He's not a savage," I blurted out. "Ya shouldn't call him that."

"Why not...?" Jason asked, not sounding put off by my statement, but truly interested in the subject.

"He doesn't even speak English," Jenny said.

"Lots of people don't speak English. That doesn't make them bad people. Being different doesn't mean you're bad."

They both looked as if they were muddling this information in their minds. Jenny ran her tiny fingers across a doily atop the dresser. "Have you got a name for the baby?" she asked shyly, not looking at me.

"I hadn't thought about it," I said, surprised as they were I hadn't.

Just then, their mother called out for them from across the house. "Jason...Jenny."

"We've got to go. Don't tell anyone we were here," Jason said, rushing for the door.

"I like the name Beatrice," Jenny said, smiling at me.

"What if it's a boy?" I asked.

The question seemed to throw her.

"Come on," Jason said, pulling his sister out the door by her sleeve.

✳✳✳✳✳✳✳✳

It became our nightly routine. After they washed and dressed for bed, just before their mother came up to tuck them in, Jason and Jenny visited me in my room.

They were inquisitive, constantly asking questions. Mostly, they asked about what it was like to be black and to be a slave. It was a learning experience for all of us. I'd answer their questions as best I could. It surprised me how little they knew about us. They weren't stupid, just ignorant, raised that way, kept that way by their parents and the adult world they came in contact with. I was what they were always warned about.

One night, Jason asked, "Does it feel different to have black skin?"

"I don't know how to answer that," I said. "I've got nothin' to compare it to, since I've always been this color. I suspect, it don't feel no different to me than it does for y'all to be white."

"May I touch it?" Jenny asked.

I put out my arm. She ran her fingers up and down from wrist to elbow.

"It's so smooth," she exclaimed, sounding surprised.

"I'll tell ya what does feel different. The way people treat ya because your skin is black."

"But isn't that the way it's supposed to be," Jason stated as factual.

"What if people treated y'all different because you're white, treating ya bad because you're white?"

"That's not supposed to happen," he countered, feeling threatened. "The Good Book says to treat everyone like you want to be treated."

"I think ya just answered your own question," I smiled.

This affected them deeply, I could tell. We would have delved deeper, but they ran to their room when they heard the sound of their mother's footsteps on the stairs.

Weeks later, the child growing within me was unmistakably showing, the children's questions switched to that of babies. This was a difficult subject to talk to them about. I wanted to be straightforward and honest; nevertheless, there were certain areas of the subject I felt weren't mine to disclose to young minds. So, I kept my answers true, although often a bit vague.

"Is the baby going to be black?" Jenny asked.

"Yes, the father is black and I am, too. That's how it works."

She continued to question, "Does it hurt to have the baby in you?"

"Sometimes it gets uncomfortable, especially, when he moves around."

"He moves around?" they both asked, sounding amazed.

"Of course, he does. He's a baby. How would ya feel if ya was stuck in a small space for nine months?"

"Go ahead, make him move," Jenny said, staring at my belly.

"Oh, I can't make him move. He moves when he wants to move," I laughed. "Here, place your hand here. If ya wait long enough, ya can feel him move."

Jenny reached out slowly, as if she were putting her hand into the fire. Her hand rested on my belly.

"I don't feel anything," she said.

"Just ya wait."

Suddenly, the baby moved. Surprised, Jenny pulled her hand back quickly.

"I felt him...I felt him," she cheered.

She placed her hand on me, again.

"He's moving," she whispered. "I can feel him moving. Jason, I can feel him moving. You need to feel him, Jason."

"I don't think we should be doing this," he said firmly. He took hold of his sister's hand, guiding her out the door. "Come, Jenny, we need to get into bed before mother suspects something."

****

It had been a long day working in the kitchen. Being on my feet all-day in my condition did me in, leaving me with a hurting back. For the first time ever, I couldn't wait to get upstairs to my room.

I must have fallen asleep. I found myself on the bed, still in my clothes. What woke me was the sound of my bedroom door opening. I looked up expecting to see Jason and Jenny in their nightgowns. Instead, what I saw brought me fearfully to my feet, standing at the side of my bed. It was Amy Gethen, the madam of the house.

"My husband invited you to stay with us till you have your baby. He sees this as a way of insuring his investment in that savage. He wouldn't bring one of his prized cows into the house to pass a calf; I don't know why this is any different. I don't like you here. I don't want you here. But my husband does, and I try my best to comply with his wishes."

I knew where she was taking this. I remained silent, doing my best not to make eye contact, fearing I'd rile her, making matters worse.

She continued, "This is my house as well as it is his. If you are going to stay with us, while you're here, I don't want to hear or see you. But most of all, I don't want you anywhere near my children.

"I don't want you to talk with them. I don't want them alone with you in this room. I will speak with them both to tell them the same. I don't know how this started, but I want it to stop right now. Do you understand?"

Afraid to speak, I just nodded.

Again, she went on, "If you disobey me, even to the slightest degree. I will see that you and your baby are turned out to die in the fields. I don't care how much my husband's invested in all this."

I remained standing, staring at the floor, afraid to look up.

"I don't want my babies in contact with coloreds."

"Yes, ma'am," I said softly.

"I didn't hear that," she insisted.

"Yes, ma'am," I said louder.

She stormed out of the room.

I shook with nervousness as I prepared for bed.

The next morning, while walking down the stairs, on my way to the kitchen, I met up with Jenny.

"Good morning, Audean," she smiled.

"Good morning, Miss," I said abruptly, trying to ignore her.

"Audean, what's the matter?" she asked.

"Jenny, it's no good. We must never speak to each other, again, or your mother will hurt me and my child."

She looked at me, seemingly offended. "That's not true. My mother would never do that."

I realize what I needed to say though it hurt me to say it. "You're right, Jenny, your mother would never hurt anyone. It was just a bad joke. I'm sorry. Still, your mother thinks it's not a good thing for white children to speak with coloreds. You need to always obey your mother."

Jenny looked at me through hurt eyes.

I quickly turned, heading for the kitchen. Just in time, too, or she would have seen the tears in my eyes.

Twenty

Her Name is Nzuri

As my delivery day approached, Gethen relieved me of my kitchen duties, which was just as well. I became useless. I waddled around like a duck. I couldn't lift, bend, or stand for very long. Wisely by Gethen, I was ordered to my bed for the remaining days.

The good part was the gap between my mother and I disappeared, and she was the one who crossed it. Delivering my meals three times a day, we began talking. In no time the relationship we once had was now ours, again. I also think my having a baby connected us even more. Besides, being mother and daughter, we began talking woman to woman. It was more than I could hope for. If I ever loved my mother, that love grew to new proportions.

In the slave quarters there were three midwives. All three Gethen put on notice, each of them checking on me everyday. It was clear they didn't want anything to do with me. Nevertheless, not wanting to disobey Massa, they came.

*∗∗∗∗∗∗∗∗

It was late in the night when the pains began. One of the midwives came to check on me.

"It's time. Tonight's the night," she said, and then she sent word for the other two midwives to come. Thankfully, they sent word for my mother. When she arrived, I knew everything would be all right. Having her at my bedside was to me like a lighthouse guiding me out of dangerous waters to a safe harbor.

Everything was as I was told it would be. It was everything I imagined it would be, except for the pain that was beyond that. The spasms of pain came and went. With each passing hour, they grew closer, longer, and more intense. By midnight, I was howling to wake the dead.

Mama stayed at my side every minute, holding my hand, wiping my brow, talking me through it.

"Breathe, baby, ya got to keep breathing deep. It'll help ya. Y'all be all right, y'all get through it. Ya ain't the first and ya ain't gonna be the last. It's been done before. Ya gonna get through it."

"Did it hurt this much when ya had me?" I asked.

"I reckon so."

I looked her in the eyes.

"Thank ya, Mama."

She smiled love on me.

Just then, there was a pounding on the bedroom door. Mama rushed to answer it. Opening the door, all of us could see the madam of the house standing in the doorway in her nightgown. She looked none too pleased.

"Make her quiet down. She's scaring my babies."

"Yes'um, ma'am, we be tryin' to."

"Well, see that she does!" she shouted, slamming the door.

I didn't understand, madam of the house or not, she had two children. She knew what I was going through. How did she expect me to do what she couldn't? I thought the woman insensitive and perhaps a bit insane.

Mama sat on the edge of the bed. She took the corner of my blanket, placing it in my mouth.

"Here ya go, hon, bite down hard on this."

I couldn't believe we were catering to the whims of that woman.

I could hear her in the hallway, arguing with her husband, the sound of Jason and Jenny shrieking in the night. For their sake and my mother's, I bit down hard on the blanket, trying to keep my moans deep in my throat.

I couldn't tell how much time passed. It was surely after midnight, still dark, a few hours before morning, when one of the midwives shouted.

"Here it comes," she announced.

"Push, baby, push," Mama told me.

I was too far gone, deep in pain to mind her or anyone or anything else.

Then I felt myself empty like an ocean wave flowing out of me. Instantly, a baby's cry filled the room. Then I heard those words.

"It's a girl."

God forgive me. My heart sank when I heard one of the midwives announce I'd given birth to a girl. I should have been pleased, but I knew what it meant. Gethen would not approve. He wanted a boy. A girl was only another mouth to feed, the mouth of someone unable to do any heavy labor, which was his plan. The hope for any peace in our lives, the possibility of Kujenga and I having a future, quickly went up in smoke by those three little words - *It's a girl.*

||*|*|*|*|*|*

The baby and I slept the day away. It was the next morning; I was lying in bed nursing the child. It was easy to know who the father was; she looked so much like Kujenga, as well as being one of the largest newborn babies I'd ever seen.

Gethen burst in the bedroom.

99

"I want you out of here, today!" he demanded.

I didn't say anything. I knew he was mad and I knew why.

"I'm tired of playing games with this savage. He better start fathering – boys, that is, or I'll have him killed. I swear it. I'd rather see him dead; throw my money to the wind, than me being made a fool of by some savage."

He stormed out of the room, slamming the door behind him. I thought him as insane as his wife.

When I finished nursing, the door opened again. It was Jason and Jenny.

"We come to see the baby," Jason declared.

They walked up to the edge of the bed.

"What is it?" Jenny inquired.

"It's a girl," I replied.

"Oh, good, I'm glad it's a girl," Jenny was ecstatic. "Are you going to name her Beatrice?"

"Maybe," I said. "But, I'd rather share the naming with the father."

"That man in the barn?" Jason asked.

"Yes, with Kujenga. He is the father. It's only right he has a say in this. That's where I need your help."

They looked at me confused, though excited.

"I have to go back to my parents' home. I have to take the baby. I'm not allowed to go into the barn. Kujenga deserves to see his daughter. Ya can help me by keeping your parents away from the west side of your home, so I can go into the barn. Will ya do this for me?"

"Do we have to lie? It's not right to lie," Jason announced.

"Ya don't have to lie, but if ya can keep your parents at the dining table during lunch, I can sneak into the barn."

They were silent for a moment, obviously, thinking about it.

"All right, we'll do it." Jason reassured me. They left the room, walking backwards, never taking their eyes off the newborn child until they were in the hall.

It was then my mother entered the room.

"Lunch for the Gethen family is already cooked. Dolly will be serving it."

Hearing the name *Dolly* surprised me.

"Dolly has been helping me in the kitchen since ya been gone. I've been given permission to help ya move back home. Get your stuff ready. He wants ya out right away."

I smiled at my mother. I held the baby up to her.

"This is your grandbaby," I said, holding her out.

Mama slowly reached out, taking her in her arms.

"She's a big ole girl, ain't she?" Mama said.

We both laughed, and then a moment later began to cry. We laughed as we cried.

****

Leaving the main house from the kitchen, we headed home. It was slow and difficult for me. It was uncomfortable to walk. As we passed the front of the barn, I stopped, staring at the door.

"Ain't no sense in wishing for what can never be, "Mama said, pushing me along.

Then I thought that if Jason and Jenny were doing what I'd asked of them, I could visit with Kujenga. And they were doing what they promised. Over lunch they kept their parents occupied by asking a hundred and one questions.

I walked to the barn door, opening it.

"Audean, don't," my mother called to me, and then holding her breath.

As with many times before, between Kujenga and me, no words were needed. He stood before us, chained like an animal. Still, his eyes shone like any other proud father's. I held the child out to him. He took her up in his arms. Looking down on the bundle, he began to cry.

"Nzuri," he whispered. He looked up into my eyes. Nzuri," he repeated, and then handed her back to me.

"Nzuri," I echoed to be sure I pronounced the name correctly. "Nzuri," I repeated, smiling at Kujenga. I had no idea what the word meant, but it sounded beautiful.

Though I knew he didn't understand, I still had to formally say it. "This is your daughter. This is your daughter, Nzuri."

He smiled at both of us in agreement.

I slowly backed away until my back hit the barn door. Sorrowfully, I turned and left.

Outside, I found my mother still standing there, looking relieved that we hadn't gotten caught.

"Come, Audean, before someone sees us."

"Mother," I said sternly, handing the baby to her. Mama took her in her arms ever so gently, smiling down on the child. "Mother, this is your granddaughter, Nzuri."

"But, that's an African name. The master won't allow it," she said with fear.

I repeated, "This is your granddaughter, Nzuri."

At our home, we found Papa on the front porch sitting in his rocking chair. He stood to greet us. I didn't say a word. I just handed him his granddaughter. He sat back down, rocking for an hour, silently holding his grandchild. Finally, he looked up at me with sorrowful eyes.

"Her name is Nzuri," I announced.

Papa smiled. This seemed to please him.

Twenty-One

Unforeseen

Thankfully, there were a few older women in the slave quarters who were no longer strong enough to put in a full day in the fields, but had not outlived their usefulness. They remained in the slave quarters all-day taking care of the children too young for plantation work, allowing their parents to labor without worry for their children. Though, women of young babies, such as me, they allowed a longer lunch period to be able to nurse their children.

I was back working in the kitchen with my mother. Despite the underlying sadness in my life, some things were never so good. My mother and I were closer than ever. We spoke intimately about our lives and feelings. Many were the day we laughed and cried together. No longer just parent and child, but now close friends.

Deidra and Lucius matured by the happenings going on around them. Being an aunt and uncle was not only pleasing to them, but gave them a sense of responsibility, which they carried out joyfully.

As for my father, having a grandbaby softened him. Like clockwork, each night after supper he would sit on the porch in his rocking chair with Nzuri in his arms. I'd be in the kitchen helping my mother clean up and I'd hear him singing gently to her, lullabies and even church hymns. This surprised me, affecting me deeply. I'd never seen this side of my father. He was always a gentle man, though never one for sentimentality.

One night, he surprised me. I came out onto the porch to get Nzuri.

"I need to get her to bed, Papa."

He looked up at me with the saddest eyes.

"He's all right, Audean"

At first I didn't know what he was talking about, and then it dawned on me he spoke about Kujenga. In all the time he brought Kujenga his supper, Papa never mentioned him to me, no matter how much I begged him to.

"He's all right. He works hard in the fields. No one bothers him. He stays to himself. At night, when I bring him his meals, he seems nice enough. We don't talk, of course, but he seems nice enough."

"Thank ya, Papa."

"Thank ya," he whispered, handing Nzuri to me.

Then there was Nzuri. What can I say? Asking a mother about their child is like picking flowers for a boutique. She was so precious with the face of a cherub. Those small puckered lips, round cheeks, and the longest lashes. Even being that young, her personality shone bright. If she cried, you had better listen for she only cried when there was good cause to, stopping immediately once remedied.

****

We just finished cooking and serving lunch at the main house for the Gethen family. I was leaving to go to the slave quarters to nurse Nzuri. When I walked out the backdoor, it surprised me to come face-to-face with of all people, Dolly.

"Can we talk?" she asked. There was a gentle humility in her voice that intrigued me to stop and listen.

She moved about nervously, staring at the ground, avoiding eye contact.

"I figured someone needed to tell ya what's goin' on," she continued. "I know how ya feel about the boy in the barn. I thought ya wanted to know. The Massa ordered every young girl to sleep with your fella. He wants us to have babies by him."

"But most of them are married," I stated.

"It don't matter none to the Massa. He don't care. He just wants babies."

"Kujenga would never do that," I insisted.

"If he don't, Massa will have all our hides. Any young girl who don't have a baby by him within the next year is gonna be in big trouble. Ya gotta talk to your boyfriend."

"What am I supposed to say to him? That he has my permission to sleep with every young girl on the plantation?"

"Yes," she answered. "I know it shocks ya, but that's the truth. Massa got it in his head he wants African babies. He's paid big money, and he wants babies. Now, if ya care about anyone's life but your own, ya gotta do this."

"I'll think about," I said.

"Well, think about it quick like, 'cause I'm supposed to spend the night in the barn tomorrow."

****

Working in the fields was always difficult for Kujenga, what with the hard work; the cruel treatment by the overseers, and the cold distance of the other slaves, except, now it grew worse.

Word got around of Gethen's plan for every young slave girl to be impregnated by the savage. The eligible young women gave him side-glances of fear. No woman wants to be told who to love or whose baby they should carry.

The families of these girls looked down on Kujenga as a threat, a savage they did not want to mix their blood with. The thought of a grandchild by this beast angered them.

Still, this was nothing compared to the anger in the eyes of the husbands and boyfriends of these young women. They wanted him dead at any cost. It was only a matter of time that one of them tried to kill him. They, themselves, would rather be dead than have their women disgraced in such a manner. A real man would never let any such thing happen. It wasn't long before someone tried to take Kujenga's life.

Word in the slave quarters was that Dolly was to spend the night, if not many, in the barn with the savage. All knew for what ends and purposes. This did not sit well with Kendall. If you remember, Kendall was the father of Dolly's child. They never married. Dolly and her child, a fine looking boy, lived with her parents. He never stepped up to claim either woman or child. Still, at least in his own mind, he felt Dolly to be his woman. The thought of her being with another man set him afire. Madness took over him; one he never knew existed.

He had a plan to kill the savage, the same day Dolly was scheduled for the barn that night. It wasn't a good plan, then again, he wasn't thinking clearly. He was running on nothing but raw emotion.

It was common for the overseers to watch over the slaves as they ate their midday meal out in the fields. When the slaves finished, only then would the overseers eat theirs. They'd position themselves sitting on the ground where they could see the working slaves. Besides their holstered pistols, each overseer had a rifle or a shotgun. Seated on the ground, holding their meal plates was one of the few times they put their arms down on the ground next to them. That was part of Kendall's plan.

Everyone was working, including Kujenga who was standing alone. Kendall rushed one of the overseers, picking up his shotgun from off the ground. Before anyone could do anything, Kendall ran across the field toward Kujenga, firing the shotgun, blasting him square in his chest. In the blink of an eye, two things happened. Kujenga crashed to the ground like a ragdoll. The overseers jumped to their feet, pulled their side arms, each firing no less than three shots into Kendall. Smoke and the smell of gunpowder filled the air. Kendall was dead before he hit the ground.

They checked, Kujenga was still breathing. Hackett ordered two of the overseers to take Kujenga to the barn, while he went to tell Gethen.

"I want you to ride like the devil into town and bring back Doc Majors."

"But, sir..." Hackett complained.

"I want that savage alive!" Gethen shouted. "Do you know how much he cost me? I want him alive."

Both Hackett and Gethen knew it was no longer the money. Furcas Gethen wanted to prove to the world he was in charge, not the overseers, nor the slaves, not even God.

****

Doctor Robert Majors was an aging southern gentleman, well-dressed; every hair on his head and in his beard was snow-white. A short man, who'd become even shorter, losing two inches of height over the last ten years. He'd known Furcas Gethen since he was just a boy. Often, he'd stepped into the fatherly role with Furcas, acting as a confidant, which is why the doctor held no qualms about entering the library without being asked and pouring himself a brandy.

"Will he live?" Gethen asked.

"What do you care?" Majors said, taking the first sip of his brandy.

"He's cost me a lot of money."

Majors laughed, "Since when do you care about money, Furcas?"

Gethen didn't want to go down that path by himself, least of all with the old man who knew him better than anyone else in the world, including his wife.

"Will he live?" Gethen repeated.

"It's hard to say. I've taken all the buckshot out of his chest. It's out of my hands, now; it's in God's. Oh, that's right, you don't like such talk. Sorry. Well, he might live. He's young, strong, and as big as a house. He's got that going for him, at least," Majors said, finishing his brandy in one gulp and then pouring another.

****

It was all the talk in the slave quarters that night.

Dolly was relieved in more than one way. She would not have to spend the night in the barn. The other reason was, though she'd never admit to anyone, she no longer had to contend with Kendall, who she always thought of as a pestering bore. For appearance's sake, she did cry a few tears.

As for me, I walked about the house, rocking Nzuri in my arms, both of us crying.

"Now, now, child, ya need to stop your crying for both of your sakes, go to bed and try to get some sleep," Mama advised.

Again, my father's actions surprised me, touching my heart.

"Don't worry, Audean. Tomorrow, when I take him his meal, I'll check on him for ya."

"Tell him I love him," I whimpered.

"How am I supposed to do that?" Papa asked.

"He understands the word *love*, and he knows my name. Just say, 'Audean love'. He'll understand.

The next night, when my father came home from bringing Kujenga's meal to the barn, I ran out onto the porch to greet him.

"Is he all right? Did ya give him my message?" I pleaded.

He looked up at me in sadness. "I'm sorry, darlin'. He's still out cold."

Twenty-Two

One More Brave Step

Strangely enough, many slaves would rather remain slaves. Oh, they will tell you they'd run away in a second if given the chance. That is true for most. Still, there are many who are afraid of the outside world. Slavery is all they know, it is all they have ever known. If they did run, where would they go, what would they do when they got there? All these misgivings outweighed thoughts of freedom, a freedom they had never known.

Also, running is dangerous. It may cost you your life. Many have responsibilities, husbands, wives, elders, and children. It is a big decision to run. And then there was talk of the Underground Railroad. Was it real? And if it was, could you rely on it. It certainly wasn't without risk.

Taking this all into consideration, you could never imagine anyone risking their life to become a slave. Yet, that is exactly what happened at the Gethen Plantation.

No one knew who she was, where she came from, or where she disappeared to at the end of each day. She was just there one day, working beside everyone in the fields.

She was an old black woman, petite and frail. She was familiar with work on a plantation. She kept up with the best of them. Her deep wrinkled skin not only a testament to her age but also was a sure sign she spent years in the fields. Most notable was her forehead that bore a long deep scare that could be seen from many feet away. One could only imagine it was not from an accident, but rather put there by someone acting in angry hatred.

She would magically appear in the mornings, and then disappear at the end of the day like a ghost.

Just as they did with Kujenga, they ignored her. No one approached or spoke to her. The overseers thought she was just another of the hundred-plus slaves. So many come and go, the faces blend into one.

It was a good thing that they never counted heads at the beginning of the day or at the end. They would have been long on the first count and short on the second.

The mystery was not only where did she come from. What they feared most was who she was. Most folk would denounce her as 'not one of us', but a stranger, not to be trusted. Perhaps, a dream shared by many, or worse. Superstition dictates a witch, an evil spirit, or even the soul of a slave who died on the plantation many years ago, not at rest and still showing up to put in a day's work.

\|\|*\|*\|*

Born into slavery, Minty was a rebel, thus the scar on her forehead. One of her masters, as there were many during her early life, heaved a two-pound weight at her, hitting her in the head for disobedience. Minty was sixteen years old when this happened, from that day on dizziness and pain plagued her.

Minty's life was no different from most slaves in Maryland. She was one of nine children raised by their mother, Rit, and father, Ben. Raised on the Good Book, they were a tight knit family. It tore Minty's heart to shreds when her three sisters, Linah, Mariah Ritty, and Soph were sold to other slaveowners. She would never see or hear from them again. It was then she vowed to fight slavery tooth and nail or die. This promise was the cause of much sorrow. Keeping fully dressed, showing only a hint of skin; even in the heat of summer working in the fields to hide the many lashes across her back and arms was part of her way of life.

Minty married a young man named John, for what purpose unknown to friends and family. John was a shy, timid man, with no desire or backbone to be free, which was Minty's daily focus. For this reason, they did not stay together long.

It was at this time, Minty learned she was to be sold along with her two brothers to another plantation. After the heartbreak of separation from her sisters for life, she was determined to not go gently with the flow of this cold-blooded river.

On the sly, Minty grew vegetables on the sides of her house, selling them, and pocketing the money. When she felt she had enough, she planned to runaway to the freedom of the North. Legend has it, before leaving, Minty passed by the window of her parents' home where Rit and Ben sang her good-bye with a chorus of *I'm bound to leave you, bound for Jordan on the other side.*

Up North, she did what she could to make a living. She would often attach herself to a plow, pulling it to make a few rows, proving to local farmers she was as strong as any man, or horse, for that matter. She never was without work.

When she saved enough money she bought a small farm in Auburn, New York. It was a huge success. Still, her hatred for slavery coursed her life. She became part of the Underground Railroad. Celebrated by the northern abolitionists for helping more than three-hundred slaves flee over the Mason/Dixon line, some even into to Canada, she was considered a heroine.

Though her crowning achievement was buying her parents out of slavery, and then moving them to her farm in Auburn, New York, where they finished their days free and happy.

Now, she'd taken one more brave step to free another slave, Kujenga, fulfilling the promise made to her friend and comrade, Treven Gilley.

****

Of all people, it was my father who finally unraveled the mystery of the stranger. It was at the end of the day when the sun is nearing the horizon, when shadows are long, and the overseers are moving the slaves from the fields to their quarters. Papa looked across the field. He saw the old woman walking toward the forest in the distance. Not being one to be easily spooked or superstitious like some of the others, he ran to catch up with her.

Hearing his footsteps behind her, she turned to face him. He stopped his running, standing before her.

"Ah, just the man I wanted to see," she announced.

Shivers ran up and down Papa's spine. He thought he was the one pursuing her. Instead, it was she who sought him out. He was part of her plan and didn't even know it. He was speechless.

"You're the one who brings the meals to the African boy in the barn?"

"Yes, I bring the savage his food," Papa replied, hesitantly.

"Don't call him that," the old woman scolded. "Would ya call your grandpa a savage? He came from the old country, too. It's a big world. Not everyone can be like ya is. All be the creation of the same God, deserving respect."

Papa hadn't felt this kind of shame since he was just a boy with his mother slapping his wrist, putting him in his place.

"My name's Minty."

"I'm Joseph."

"Well, Joseph, you're gonna get me in to see this boy."

"I don't understand," Papa said.

"I made a dying promise to a friend I'd free this boy."

"But he can't speak a lick of English."

"So what...?"

"Well, he could be dead by the end of the day. A few days ago, he got himself shot, a shotgun, peppered him all in his chest. He ain't lookin' none too good."

Minty shook her head. "That is a problem. But I still want to see him. Let's meet here tomorrow this same time, and ya can bring me to him."

Minty turned, starting again for the forest.

"Where y'all stayin'?" Papa asked.

"In the woods," she called back.

"Do ya need anything?"

"That's kind of ya, but I got all I need. Just do what I say."

****

108

The next day, Papa kept an eye out for Minty. She never showed, a fact gone unnoticed by the overseers, a relief to many of the slaves. Still, some worried all the more that she wasn't there.

At the end of the day, Papa did as he was told, waiting in the field facing the forest.

"Are ya ready?" Minty's voice sounded behind him. He jumped with fright, spinning in the air, coming down, facing her.

"Dang, ya scared the bejeezus outta me."

"Sorry. Now, take me to the boy."

"I gotta go to the kitchen at the main house, first, to get his supper."

Papa started for the main house, Minty followed close behind.

At the back of the main house, Papa stopped at the kitchen door.

"Ya better let me go in by myself. I don't think I can explain ya to my wife and daughter."

"Best they don't know," Minty agreed.

The Bible talks about married couples becoming one flesh, my parents were prime examples of this. When my mother itched, my father scratched, and visa versa. So, when my father entered the kitchen, with just one look my mother knew something was wrong.

"Joseph, are ya all right?"

"I'm fine, just a bit tired," Papa answered, trying to avoid eye contact.

"I know tired when I see tired. There's something else wrong with ya. Come here, let me touch ya forehead, see if ya got a fever."

"Woman, I told ya I'm tired. Can't a man be tired without women folk pawin' at them?"

Mama rolled her eyes, letting out a long sigh. She handed him the plate, Kujenga's supper. There were never any utensils...too dangerous. Kujenga ate with his hands.

"Audean and I are goin' to the house. When ya bring back the plate, leave it on the table. We'll get it in the mornin'."

I moved in closer. "Papa, when ya see Kujenga tell him I love him."

Mama laughed, "Your father has a hard time speakin' what he knows, let alone some African jibber jabber."

I just smiled at Papa. He knew what to say.

"Say, what's goin' on between the two of ya?" Mama asked, sounding suspicious.

"Ya sure are the pushy one, tonight," Papa said, taking the plate from my mother. Before he left, he turned to give me a wink.

When he'd gone, my mother removed her apron, tossing it on the table. She had that look on her face I'd seen before whenever she was cross with my father. I knew what that look meant. This was one wife who would not be speaking to her husband that night.

As they approached the barn, Papa looked around frantically.

"If anyone sees us, the overseers or someone in the house, we need to split up, maybe try another day. If we get caught, we're both dead."

Minty didn't seem concerned, leaving the decision up to my father to make the call.

He opened the barn door slightly ajar, pushing Minty through the opening, and then following.

Kujenga was flat on his back, still feeling the ill affects of the gun blast. He could do no more than raise his head and open his eyes to see who it was.

Minty rushed to him, falling to her knees at his side, she placed her hand on his shoulder.

"Weka bado," she whispered, holding him down.

Kujenga's eyes went wide to hear his native tongue.

"Ya can speak his language?" Papa asked, amazed.

"A little," Minty replied, "just enough to get me in trouble."

"Minty," she said, identifying herself.

"Kujenga," he said in reply.

She reached down into the deep pockets of her skirt, bringing out a flat jar. She unbuttoned the front of Kujenga's shirt. Opening the jar, there was a thick white cream. She dipped two fingers into the salve.

"Weka bado," she repeated.

She began smearing the salve over the wounds on his chest.

"He's lucky," she said. "He was shot with a scattergun, lots of little pellets that don't go too deep, as opposed to fewer thick pellets that tear ya apart. He'd be dead now, if they did. I guess they use scatter shells to stop a slave but not kill him. Don't want to waste good money on a workin' slave, if ya don't have to."

It was clear the slightest touch on his wounds tortured Kujenga, yet he grit his teeth, remaining silent.

"That's a brave boy. That's my brave boy," Minty murmured. She looked to my father, "I came to rescue him, only he can't be moved."

"Will he live?" asked Papa.

"As long as these wounds don't get infected, he's got a good chance. He's young, healthy as a horse and as strong as a bull. But he can't be moved for a long time. I can't stay here; I'll be back in a few months." Closing the jar, she handed it to Papa. "Here, I want ya to rub a little on his wounds everyday. It'll keep away the infection."

"Like hell I will!" Papa replied, refusing to take the jar. "This savage deflowered my daughter, Audean, and gave her a baby. It's hard enough having to bring this bastard his meal, everyday. I'll be damned if I'll be his nursemaid! If it were up to me, I'd see him dead and buried."

Minty stared at Papa for a long time before saying a word.

"Joseph, that's a Christian name. Are ya a Christian?"

Papa took a long time to answer, "Yes, I am. What about it?"

"Then ya know what the Good Book says. It says to love ya enemies. Well, if this boy is your enemy, then ya better start showin' him some love. That baby your daughter had, what was it, a boy or a girl?"

"A girl, her name is Nzuri."

Kujenga stirred at the mention of his daughter's name.

"Do ya love that child?"

"Of course, I do. She's my grandbaby."

"Well, this man is the cause of your joy. Don't the Bible say that God works in mysterious ways, and for all things to turn out good in the long run? Well, it sounds like ya got more of the good out of it than sorrow. Ya got a healthy daughter and grandbaby out of the deal. Ya should be grateful. Christian? My eye..."

A wave of shame washed over my father. Just then, Minty took hold of Papa's arm, placing his hand next to Kujenga's arm.

"What color is this hand?" she said. "What color is this boy's arm? They're the same color. Like it or not, that makes ya brothers. Ya is brothers in the spirit, in God's eyes, and ya is brothers in the flesh, in the eyes of the world. Now, ya take this salve, and ya do what I tells ya," she scolded.

Once Papa took the jar, Minty smiled.

"Now, step outside for a minute. I need to talk to this boy, alone. I'll be out soon."

Papa left the dinner plate on the ground next to Kujenga, putting the jar in his pocket, he left the barn.

It was many years later that I learned what occurred in that barn between Minty and Kujenga.

With her limited vocabulary, Minty tried to learn Kujenga's story, from his capture thousands of miles away to his life in the barn. Most of what she learned was about me and the baby. Audean and Nzuri were the words repeated from his lips. His concern for us was an unbearable burden for him.

Again, with the few words that she knew, she told him he must get well, and when he did she would come back for him to lead him to freedom. It became clear he understood her, but what was also clear, was he would not leave without his two loves, Audean and Nzuri. Minty agreed, vowing she would come up with a plan that all three of us would escape.

Once they settled on those points, Minty, again, reached into her deep pockets, taking out a long metal file. She ran it a few times over a link in Kujenga's chain, leaving a mark in the steel. He nodded that he understood what it was for. Using the file, Minty dug a deep, short burrow in the dirt. She placed the file in the burrow, covering it up. They both understood it would be used at a later time.

Before she could rise to her feet, Kujenga reached out, taking her hand. "Love," he whispered, being one of the few English words he knew.

"I love ya, too, my brother."

She rose to her feet, tiptoeing out of the barn.

Outside, she found Papa worriedly standing guard.

"If that boy dies, I'm gonna hold ya completely responsible," Minty warned him.

"What are ya sayin'? I'll put the damn salve on him. But if he dies, it won't be my fault."

"There's one other thing ya need to do." Minty waited till she was sure she had his full attention. "I want ya to talk to ya daughter. Tell her how he's doin' in there. Tell her that he loves her and their daughter. She needs to hear that."

Papa let out a long sigh. "Anything else?" he asked, sarcastically.

"I'll be back in a month. He should be healed by then."

"Or dead..." Papa interrupted.

Minty ignored him, continuing, "I'll be back in a month."

She started to walk off and turned back, looking at him.

"Joseph?"

"Yes?"

"Thank ya."

He didn't expect that, nor suspected how good it made him feel.

Minty turned, walking off. The sun had nearly fallen below the horizon. The sky was a burst of red and orange. While my father admired the sunset, he didn't notice Minty had disappeared.

****

That evening seemed just like all the evenings before it. While, Deidra and Lucius played in their bedroom, Mama and I cleaned up the kitchen, while Papa rocked in his rocking chair on the front porch, holding Nzuri in his arms.

I was just about to step out onto the porch when I stopped to listen. Papa was softly singing to Nzuri.

MY LITTLE COLORED CHILD *

A snow-white stork flew down from the sky
Rock-a-bye, my baby bye
To take a baby gal so fair

To a young missus, waitin' there
When all was quiet as a mouse
In ole Massa's big fine house

Dat little gal was born rich and fair
She's de sap from out a sugar tree
But ya are just as sweet to me
My little colored child
Just lay ya head upon my breast
And rest, ya rest, ya rest, ya rest
My little colored child

To a cabin in a woodland dear
Ya come by a mammy's heart to cheer
In this ole slave's cabin
Your hands my heartstrings grabbin'
Just lay your head upon my breast
Just snuggle and rest and rest
My little colored child

Ya daddy plows ole Massa's corn
Ya mammy does the cookin'
She'll give dinner to her hungry child
When nobody is a lookin'
Don't be ashamed, my child, I beg
'Cause ya was hatched from a buzzard's egg,
My little colored child

It was then I realized my mother stood by my side. She placed her hand on my shoulder.

"He's a good man, Audean, don't ever sell him short."

I stepped out onto the porch, pretending I hadn't heard a word.

"Time for bed, Nzuri," I said, reaching out.

Papa held out Nzuri to me. I took her in my arms, starting back into the house, when he called to me.

"Audean…?"

"Yes, Papa…?"

He looked up from his rocking chair with sorrowful eyes.

"Audean, your man is doin' better, I believe he is gonna live. He and I don't talk much." He chuckled under his breath, knowing it was an obvious statement. "But I know this much. He wanted me to tell ya that he loves ya and the baby."

"Thank ya, Papa. That's very sweet of ya to tell me."

"Don't mention it," was the best he could muster.

I was just about to go back into the house when he called to me, again.

"Audean…?"

"Yes, Papa…?"

"Thank ya for bringin' Nzuri into this family. I love ya both."

"We love ya, too, Papa."

Mama was still standing in the kitchen. She held me to her, kissing me, and then Nzuri's cheek.

In the bedroom, I placed Nzuri in the center of the bed. The sweet baby was already asleep.

MY LITTLE COLORED CHILD was a well-known lullaby sung by slave families in the 1800's. Sadly, it was based on the folklore told by plantation white women to black slave children that the stork delivered white babies to the plantation; where as black babies were hatched from a buzzard's egg.

Twenty-Three

What Minty Did

Talk about an Underground Railroad was always in the air. Plantation owners would talk about it over cigars and brandy. Their wives would talk about it outside church, after Sunday service. But where it was talked about with most importance, cloaked in secrecy, was in the slave quarters.

Late at night, long after the children went to sleep; the slaves would sit in homes around blazing fireplaces, whispering stories about the Underground Railroad.

The trouble was no one knew for certain if it was real or not. Was it a myth started by hopeful souls? Had such things actually happened, but only a handful of times, and it was nothing to put your trust in?

There was no way of knowing if it was all rumors. There was no way to get in touch with the Underground Railroad. Either they got in touch with you, for there was no way you could contact them, if they existed at all.

Someone told me...I heard once...my daddy told me. Hearsay, that's all it ever was, nothing but hearsay. And no body puts their life on the line for hearsay.

Monroe Beaker was a single black man living in the communal barn with the rest of the other single men. It wasn't that he didn't try getting hitched but when it ain't in the cards, it just ain't there. Besides, Monroe liked the looks of a woman, but on every other level he could take them or leave them. That's not to mention his thoughts on children. They were fine if they belong to somebody else. Otherwise, a loyal ole hound dog was more to his liking.

One night when everyone was nice and warm, snuggled up for the night in the community barn, the barn door opened and in walked Walter Miller. He unsuccessfully tried to make his way to the back of the barn without stepping on anyone.

"Watch where ya walkin'," they shouted at Walter. Finally, he made it to the back wall, where he knew he'd find his buddy, Monroe.

"Monroe, is that ya?" he whispered.

"Of course it is. Who'd ya think it be? Why ya here and ain't in bed with Alice?"

"I came to give ya somethin'."

"What that be?"

"Keep it low, I don't want anyone else to hear," Walter whispered, handing Monroe a slip of folded paper. Unfolding it, there was just enough light in the communal barn to read it. It was a map of the surrounding area.

"What the hell's this?" Monroe asked.

"It's a map of the plantation, the forest, and the countryside, up to fifty miles from here," answered Walters.

Monroe examined the map in detail.

"I recognize these fields, the forest, and even some of these hills after that. But what's this?" he asked, pointing to an X at the top of the map."

"Every first Monday of the month, someone from the Underground Railroad waits there from noon to three for whatever slave can make it there. Then they take 'em to freedom."

Monroe continued to study the map. "I don't know where this is," he said, pointing to the X, "But it's got to be at least fifty miles from here. The dogs they sic on ya would have ya in half that time before ya got there," Monroe said circling his finger around the X.

After being made to look foolish, Walter stuck to his guns. "Ya don't know you're such a crybaby. It all looks too hard for ya, so let's just continue to be slaves and work for Satan."

"What the hell's that got to do with anything? I ain't ever seen or heard from anybody in the Underground Railroad, now ya show up with a map on how to get to 'em. What do ya think I'm supposed to believe?"

"If ya were a real man, ya'd jump at the chance."

"What the hell is that suppose to mean? If it's such a great opportunity, why ain't ya doin' it?"

"I'm married," Walter pointed out, "you're not. Alice don't want me taking any unnecessary chances with our family. We've got kids, ya know? Maybe, when their older, we'll take the chance."

"Gee, I don't know."

Walter continued to debate Monroe. "Here ya are, single, free and easy, no responsibilities in the world, and you're afraid of takin' a chance. What's the worse that could happen?"

"What's the worse that could happen?" Monroe laughed. "If I'm not killed when I'm caught, I'll be dragged back to the plantation to be killed, probably hanged or whipped to death. That's the worse that could happen."

Walter didn't put up an argument. He knew everything Monroe said was true. His disagreement took a gentler tone.

"Listen, Monroe, I could have easily given this information to my brother-in-law, but ya know how I feel about ya. You're my best friend, and I thought a chance at freedom was just your thing. Forgive me, if I made a mistake."

Walter took back the slip of paper, folding it, placing it back into his top pocket.

"Wait a minute," Monroe countered. "Did I say I wasn't grateful, if so I'm sorry. I appreciate your help. It just took me off guard. Yeah, I'd be glad to get out of this hellhole. It's just that...."

Monroe stopped midsentence, wondering how to express his inner feelings.

"It's just that I don't know who's more real, Father Christmas or the Underground Railroad. If ya believe in Father Christmas, and ya find out he ain't real, ain't a big thing, ya just don't get what ya want. If ya believe in the Underground Railroad, and ya find out it ain't real, ain't a big thing either, ya just don't get to live."

That was the bottom line, what needed consideration, the chance Monroe finally decided to take.

****

Over the next few days, Monroe memorized the map, and then he destroyed it, throwing it into the fire at night.

He hoarded as much food as he could, without starving himself. After a few days, he had a sack full of slow perishables, mostly hardtack.

Now the big question needed to be answered. When was the best time to make his escape?

Of course, nighttime was the obvious choice, late night when everyone slept. Monroe thought it should be on a night when there was no moon, he'd be harder to track, and then again, it would make it harder to move quickly. Besides, if he went without detection till morning, moonlight wouldn't come into play. He could move faster during a full moon. Still, none of that mattered very much, seeing how he had to be there on the first Monday of the month, between noon and three. With that in mind, he decided to make his run on a Saturday night.

The work schedule started late on Sunday mornings. It was out of respect for the Sabbath, they allowed the slaves to visit the black church a mile up the road. As well, the Massa and his family rode into town for church service at the white church. Another reason for a late work schedule on a Sunday was to give many of the overseers time to get past their hangovers, brought on by their Saturday night carousing in town. When all was said and done, it was well after noon before anyone was expected to do any work on Sunday. Monroe knew that if he made his escape around midnight on a Saturday night, he'd have at least a twelve hour lead on his pursuers. This was only a slight advantage, as a man on foot was no match for a group of men on horseback following his scent with a half dozen bloodhounds.

Speaking of bloodhounds, these dogs were not just any variety, nor did they receive training in the manner one would think of training such a dog. They lived well with plenty of acreage to run around on, and plenty of good food, far better food than what they fed to the slaves. Often, the overseers hid clothing taken from a slave at various places on the plantation and the surrounding area. Then they set the dogs loose to find the rags. It was good practice, making them more skillful, which made then worth their weight in gold to the landowner.

Now, a bloodhound's sense of smell is keen, far better than most animals, and certainly better than a human's. They also have the ability to tell different scents. They could tell animal from human, male from female, black from white. But to make the differences clearer to the hounds, desperate measures were taken. From the first day a pup was large enough to be taken from their mother, everyday they'd have a black man take a switch to them. Not hitting them hard enough to hurt them, still hard enough to sting. This would go on everyday till the dog was fully grown and ready to go on the hunt. By then, the animal could smell a black man half a mile away, and a hatred for the black man was instilled deep within them. A black man meant pain, they hated pain. So, understandably, the dogs could hunt down a runaway slave in no time. The only problem the overseers had with them was once the dogs track them down; you had to fight them off from tearing their prey limb from limb. Sometimes, they didn't bother to stop them.

<center>∗∗∗∗∗∗∗∗∗</center>

Finally, the night came for Monroe's escape. He tied the sack of food around his waist. With great care and experience not to disturb any of those sleeping on the ground, he made his way from the back of communal barn to the front door. This was far from an unusual occurrence, as the call to nature came on most folks during the night.

Outside, he found the world dark with a quietness that only happens after midnight. Looking around, he saw no one. Though he wanted to head north, he knew better than to pass by the kennel. If even one dog barked, that would wake the overseers, and someone surely would investigate. To avoid this, he left the plantation via the south of the property, When he got to the road, he turned, heading north, past the plantation. After passing the fields, he went slightly west. At the edge of the forest, he turned to the north and entered.

It wasn't a full moon night, thankfully, it was three-quarter. There was enough light pouring through the treetops to make out shapes. Still, Monroe found it rough going over rocks and felled trees, skinning his knees and elbows.

The travel was slow. When signs of sunrise filtered through the trees, he couldn't have been more than five miles away. Now that he could see better, traveling became faster. If all went as planned, he would still have five to six hours before anyone suspected anything, taking up the hunt.

Midday, Monroe came on a small creek. Crossing it, he rested, eating some hardtack, drinking from the stream. He listened carefully for the sound of dogs in pursuit, there were none. This was a good sign; still he knew it would be only a matter of time. He needed to keep his eyes peeled and ears to the ground.

North of the stream, Monroe made a sharp turn, going west. After a mile or so in this direction, he headed south, backtracking. Taking off his shoes, he waded in the water, which was only shin high. He walked through the stream, going back east. When he got to the spot he originally crossed, he continued forging east. A half mile later he stepped out of the stream on the south side. There he backtracked a quarter mile. Then he crossed, again. On the north side, once more, he put on his shoes, and again, headed north deeper into the wood. His hope was that this bizarre pattern would confuse the dogs, when they got to the stream.

Late afternoon was when Monroe heard it, the sound of angry dogs in the distance, made angrier by his antics of wading and backtracking. Monroe heard the hunting party and dogs traveling west, then east, and then west, again. He'd bought himself some precious time, how much he had no idea.

Monroe made it to high ground by nightfall. He looked back at the valley behind him. There was the far off glow of a campfire. They were closer than he'd hoped, but not going to continue in the dark. Yet, rest wasn't in the cards for Monroe. His only chance was to continue onward as fast as he could, no matter how exhausted he felt.

At sunup, he could only assume the hunting party was again tracking him down. He didn't hear dogs, which was a good sign, though it wouldn't be long before they'd be on his heels.

He needed to move faster. It was Monday morning, the first Monday of the month. He had only six or seven hours left to get to the meeting place. Would there be someone there? He could only pray. And if there was someone there, would they make themselves known, if he showed up with a party of overseers and a pack of angry dogs not far behind on his trail? The only thing he knew was that he was rushing in the right direction. How far away, he had no idea.

After going through a valley, he stopped to look up at what some might call a very high hill or what others might call a small mountain. Either way, it would be a hard climb. He could only pray the summit was the meeting place, for time was running out, he could hear dog's barking not far behind, getting closer every hour.

The slope was so steep; he huffed and puffed his way upward, scrabbling on the ground sometimes on his knees, grabbing hold of tree roots to keep moving forward and upward.

Reaching the top, he stopped to catch his breath, only to have it taken away again, when a woman snuck up behind him, scaring him half to death.

She was short, coming up to his chest. An elderly black woman who could easily pass for a grandmother, behind her stood a small donkey weighed down with supplies.

"Ya scared the bejeezus outta me!" Monroe shouted, stepping back.

The old woman didn't seem put-off in the least.

"Ya can call me Minty. What's ya name?"

"Monroe. Listen, I don't want to be disrespectful, I'm supposed to meet somebody."

"That would be me," Minty replied, sternly.

"No, ya don't understand, I'm here to meet someone from the Underground Railroad."

"That would be me," Minty repeated, this time sounding weary. "Listen, I'm it. I'm all ya got. Get it through ya head. Now, listen to me and listen good. If ya want to get out of this, do everything I tell ya."

She walked over to the donkey, bringing back some items. Just then, the sound of dog's barking echoed down in the valley below.

"Hurry up. From the sound of it, we ain't got much time. Here, put these on," she said handing him a pair of pants and a shirt. "Go on," she insisted.

"Turn ya back, please," Monroe said, shyly.

"Listen, young man, ya ain't got nothin' I ain't seen before, and probably better, now, put these on."

Monroe looked at her with sad eyes.

"All right," Minty sighed as she turned her back to him.

After a few moments, Monroe was in his new clothes.

"Ya can turn around, now," he announced.

She thought of the hundred things she'd like to call him, but there was no time.

"What should I do with my old clothes?"

"Give 'em to me."

She placed the old clothes on the ground. Again, she went to the donkey, returning with a large jar filled with what looked like black ash. She opened the jar, and began pouring the powder onto the ground on and around the clothes. After just one small whiff Monroe knew what it was.

"Black pepper...!"

"That's right, black pepper," she said, tossing the empty jar into a nearby bush. "That ought to clog up their honkers for a few hours."

Taking the donkey by the reins, Minty led them down the other side of the hill, down into the next valley. She'd obviously done this many times before, since she was surefooted, getting them down in an amazingly quick time.

As they trudge through the valley, they heard dogs barking at the summit. A moment later, they heard the sneezes of both men and beasts.

****

"I've got to stop. I can't go anymore," Monroe pleaded with Minty.

"We can't stop, now. We're almost there," she said.

"Almost where...?"

"The first station, our first stop on the Underground Railroad, we'll be there, soon."

At first, Monroe didn't understand. However, over the next few weeks he understood it fully. The Underground Railroad was an invisible path running from south to north. A trail that connected dozens of secret, safe houses, as they were called, mansions, plantations, farms, cabins, and even shacks. Each was a stop off where a slave could be safe, getting rest and food, helping them to the next safe house, on and on until they reached the Mason/Dixon Line, and over into the North.

What shocked Monroe the most was the fact that most of these safe places were owned by white folks. Not only did this surprise him, but changed his life completely. All his life whites were either owners or overseers. Some were nice, some were harsh, but none of them cared if he lived or died, always demanding something from him.

Now, wherever they went, Minty was known to them, greeting her as a friend, as they did him, also. They not only fed and gave them a place to stay, they hid them, lied for them, putting their lives in danger for them. It was truly a life changing experience for Monroe.

Once they were north of the Mason/Dixon line, Minty didn't abandon Monroe. Not knowing anyone or having a place to go, she continued to see over him like a mother hen. They continued traveling north till they came to the town of Auburn in the top portion of New York State.

There Minty owned a bit of farm property. Walking onto the property it surprised Monroe to see how many ex-slaves were there working. Minty worked out a program where slaves that came north on the Underground Railroad had a place to stay and work. The pay wasn't high, but then again there was no charge for food and lodging. Once a now-freed slave saved enough money, Minty would try to find them work in other towns, sometimes other states, even Canada. When there wasn't enough work to go around, Minty hired the workers out to nearby businesses, farms, factories, and shops.

There were two bunkhouses to lodge the workers, one large one for the men, and another smaller one for women.

All meals were served at the main house where Minty lived with her parents. You heard right, her parents. Minty being an old woman, you can only imagine how old her parents, Rit and Ben were. Good people, relaying stories of long ago, without a hint of bitterness or misgivings.

The main house was a large two-story building, not as grand as the mansion on plantations, yet homey and spacious. The dining room held a long family table, able to seat a dozen people. When there wasn't enough room at the table, they placed chairs along the walls. The men would sit at these with there plates in their laps, making sure the women had a place at the table.

It was a good life on Minty's farm; the work was hard, though no one noticed. No longer slaves, they were now working for themselves with new hope, and for once, goals in their lives.

In fact, life was so good on the farm the hardest part was when it came time to leave. But it had to be done. New runaways arrived every month. Room was needed. Everyone knew it was only fair, so when it was time to leave there were no complaints.

Monroe stayed for six months. At the end of that time, Minty escorted him into Canada, to Quebec where a job as an assistant to a well-known glassblower waited.

Over the years, Monroe's life only got better. He learned to speak French, bought a small piece of land, erecting a four-room cabin on it. In time, he became an expert glassblower, earning a high wage. The last I heard, he married, and had three children, all boys.

Twenty-Four

Born of Necessity

Word was that Kujenga was nearly recovered. In his determination, Furcas Gethen made demands on the female slave population. Every young girl married or not, was to visit the barn, a different girl each night. It bothered me to think of it. Also, what young man can resist. Sooner or later, he would give in.

Again, this brought me in contact with Dolly.

It was late at night, around the time Papa sat on the porch rocking Nzuri to sleep in his arms.

"There's someone outside wantin' to see ya," Papa said, entering the house, holding Nzuri. "Don't worry; I'll put Nzuri to bed."

"Who is it?" I asked.

"Dolly and two other girls..."

I knew what they'd come for; I took in a deep breath, sighed, walking out onto the porch.

"Can we talk wit'cha?" Dolly asked.

"Yeah, sure, what about...?"

The other two girls with Dolly were Prudence and Winnie. Like Dolly, Winnie was a young single girl, living with her folks. She was a tiny bit of a woman with bright eyes, a figure most folk would call shapely. Prudence was the same age as us, though she looked older. She was married with two babies of her own. Understandably, there was a worried look in her eyes.

"We've known one another since we were small," Winnie explains. "We don't see or talk as much as we used to. Life gets like that. We're here out of respect for ya. We know how ya feel about the boy in the barn. I mean, ya had his baby and all. And we know how he feels about ya, as well. But I'm sure ya heard what the Massa wants. He wants us to start droppin' his babies or there's gonna be hell to pay."

"What does this all have to do with me? I asked.

Dolly continued the conversation, "We just want ya to know we don't want to hurt ya, but some of us have decided to do our best to seduce your boyfriend. It's nothing personal. We're just trying to survive."

I should have expected it, but it still shocked and hurt me.

"Not all of us feel this way," Prudence added. "I know if I had another man's child, my husband would go mad. Who knows what he'd do. So, we're going to try to have a child with our husbands and say it's because of our nights spent in the barn."

"It's been tried before. Look what happened to Kendall," I said.

"Kendall had a big mouth," Dolly stated coldly. "He was a nice boy, only he liked to brag. That's why he's dead."

"I hope I can get away with it," Prudence continued. "The only thing is that if I have a child and it comes out looking nothing like the boy in the barn, the Massa will have my hide. I may just have his child and tell my husband it's his. I don't know what to do."

"His name is Kujenga," I said, nearly in tears.

"I'm sorry...Kujenga," Prudence admitted.

"What we're tryin' to say is," Winnie concluded, "we all plan to have children. Ya not gonna know which ones are Kujenga's and which ones ain't. We ain't doin' this to hurt ya, but we gotta do what's best for us and our families."

"I thought ya said ya were my friends," I pleaded.

"What would ya have us do, Audean?" Dolly argued. "Leave your precious boyfriend alone, letting Massa whip us to death."

She was right, all of us knew it.

One by one, they approached me, taking me in their arms, hugging me.

"Just remember, we love ya, girl," Prudence whispered in my ear.

****

I found myself holding Nzuri in my arms more often every night. It was so difficult to let my father rock her on the porch at night. He looked forward to it. Sometimes, I felt it was the only thing keeping him going. As for me, Nzuri was my only link to Kujenga. She was so unique. It angered me to think there would soon be others like her, born of necessity and not of love.

If only I could see Kujenga for a moment or get word to him. My father showed kindness to me by telling me of his well-being. Often at night, he would tell me that he told Kujenga of my love, giving me his response in kind. Only, Papa was too afraid. He had a wife and family to think about. The incident with Minty filled him with fear. He didn't want to go through that again. Besides, as much as he loved Nzuri and me, he hated what Kujenga had done to our lives.

And where was Minty?

There was uneasiness in the air; everyone felt it, the slaves, and the overseers. Only Furcas Gethen was oblivious to it.

Mostly, the tension came from the male slaves. They considered these women their women, not to be shared with an outsider. Their anger was twofold. They were angry with the powers that be for taking their dignity away, and they were angry with the savage who had no claim on their women. All of us knew that at some point it would all explode, especially among the married men who'd rather die than share their wives. Hackett, the head overseer, sensed this. He took no chances. He hired more men, making sure they were armed to the tooth. Each had a sidearm, a shotgun or a rifle. Hackett vowed there would be no rebellion on his watch.

****

Dolly was the first to spend a night in the barn, although she was not the last. Every day, they forced a different woman to spend the night in the barn. Were they successful in seducing Kujenga or did they fail. Instead, trying to get in the family way by the other men in the slave quarters, claiming the child was Kujenga's. There was no way of knowing what actually happened; nobody was willing to talk about it.

Prudence was the first to turn up expecting. Foolish me, in my jealousy, I had to try to learn the truth.

After putting Nzuri down to bed for the night, I snuck out of the house, making my way across the compound to Prudence's home. I knocked on the door; Prudence came out onto the porch, shutting the door behind her, lest her husband might hear.

"What are ya doin' here? What do ya want?" she whispered.

"I need to know," I begged. "The baby you're carrying is it Kujenga's or is it your husbands?"

Just then, I felt a hand gently rest on my shoulder. I spun around to see who it was. It was my mother.

"Don't do this to yourself, child. Whatever the answer is, it's only gonna hurt. Now, leave this good woman alone. Whatever her business is, it's her business and not yours. All ya need to know is your love is your love. Now, let's go home."

Mama gently guided me off the porch, towards home. She turned one last time to say goodnight.

"We're sorry about this, Prudence. Please, understand."

"No need to apologize, Mary. I fully understand. I feel for the girl."

Twenty-Five

The Savage is Loose

It was a day like any other day. All of us got up early. Mama fed her husband and children black coffee and pan-fried dough in bacon grease. Then Mama and I headed to the kitchen at the main house to cook breakfast for the Gethens, and to clean the whole day away. Papa, Deidra, and Lucius were off to the fields. It was harvesttime.

The day was long, the work was hard, but it was no different from any other day. That is until evening rolled around.

Papa came to the back door, around by the kitchen, to collect supper for Kujenga.

Mama saw him from the back window. She made up a plate of food, handing it to me.

"Here, give this to your father. I don't want him comin' in here trackin' dirt all over my nice clean floor."

I took the plate, meeting my father at the back door.

"Here's Kujenga's supper. Mama don't want ya trackin' dirt on her clean floor."

"She don't, do she?" he answered, sounding put off, taking the plate, and then walking away.

It was nearly dark. When he stepped out of the light coming from the main house, he heard a voice.

"Joseph...?" it said from behind him. It startled him so much; he threw the plate up into the air. He spun around to be face-to-face with a little old lady – Minty.

"Dang, woman, ya scared the bejeezus outta me! Ya just don't go around sneakin' up on folks like that. What'cha doin' here, anyways?"

"I said I'd be back, so here I am."

Papa picked up the scattered pieces of food off the ground, placing them on the plate.

"The string beans and taters ain't any good, but I saved him the fried chicken and cornbread," he said blowing the dirt off the chicken breast and a square of cornbread.

"I need ya to do somethin', Joseph," Minty asked politely.

"I was hopin' ya'd never come back. Now, there's goin' to be trouble for sure. All hell's broke loose since ya left. Ya being here ain't gonna make it better. Y'all probably make it worse."

I need ya to do somethin'" she continued, not to be put off by talk of danger.

"What's that?" Papa finally asked, knowing he wasn't going to get out of it.

"How's your memory?" she asked.

"What do ya mean, 'how's your memory?'."

"What do ya mean, what do I mean? Can ya remember somethin' if I tell ya?"

"Course I can."

"Well, then listen good. I goin' to tell ya somethin', I want ya to tell it to Kujenga."

"Say what?"

Minty spoke slowly and clear, "Tell him, Ni wakati."

"What the hell kind of jibber jabber is that?"

"Just say it to him. He'll understand." She repeated even slower, "Ni wakati."

"Ni wakati," Papa echoed.

"That's right. Tell him, Ni wakati."

"Ni wakati...Ni wakati...I got it, already, I got it."

Papa turned towards the barn; looking back he found Minty had vanished like the wind into the dark of night.

"Ni wakati...Ni wakati," he kept repeating so he wouldn't forget.

In the barn, Kujenga sat up when Papa entered, placing the plate on the ground before him.

"Minty," Papa said. "Minty...ya remember Minty?"

Kujenga's face lit up with recognition. "Minty...yes...Minty!"

Papa had no idea Kujenga knew the word *yes*. For the first time, the two men smiled at each other.

"Well, yes, Minty wanted me to tell you something. Now, let's see if I get this right. Ni Wakati."

Kujenga jumped to his feet.

"Ni wakati... do ya understand me?" Papa looked Kujenga up and down. "It would seem ya do."

"Ni wakati," Kujenga announced out loud.

"Yeah, well, it sounds better when y'all say it. I'll be back later for the plate."

||*|*|*|*|*

That night was like all the other nights. They brought one of the young slave girls to the barn.

"I'm not gonna tell ya what to do," Hackett told her. "I'm sure ya understand. The barn door won't be locked, but don't leave till ya did what you're brought here to do."

Afraid to speak, Clarinda nodded she understood. She was a pretty girl, but still just a child. She had just turned fifteen. It's true, many as young as she were already mothers, sometimes of two children. However, Clarinda, lacked the maturity for such things. So, her parents kept her sheltered, which was the cause of her panic, having to spend the night with a strange man, a savage, alone, in a dark barn.

The chain was around Kujenga's neck, connecting him to the main post in the barn. She felt safe enough to move around him, a few feet away, a little more than the length of the chain.

"I don't know what to do?" Clarinda cried. There were tears running down her cheeks. "I've never done this before."

Strangely enough, Kujenga smiled at her. This put her at ease. He sat down on the ground a few feet away, what she felt was a safe distance.

His smile grew larger. She smiled back.

"Now, what do we do?" she asked shyly.

"Audean..." he said. "Audean..."

"Yes, I know Audean," Clarinda replied.

Kujenga nodded his head, smiling, "Audean, yes, love, Audean."

"Yes, I knew that. Ya love Audean."

"Yes, love."

Kujenga got to his knees. With his bare hands he began digging in the dirt.

"What are ya doin'?" Clarinda asked, thinking him very strange. He looked like a dog digging for a bone.

Then he came up holding a metal file. He pointed it at Clarinda, and then at the chain around his neck, making a sawing motion.

"Oh no, I ain't helpin' ya. You're gonna get us both killed," she declared.

When he realized she wasn't going to help him, he began to grind the file across one of the links of the chain around his neck. It would take longer, and he'd have to be careful.

"Now, ya gotta stop doin' that," she insisted.

He continued, ignoring her.

Clarinda jumped to her feet. "Stop that! Someone's bound to hear. We'll both be in trouble. Either ya stop right now or I'm gonna tell someone."

Of course, Kujenga didn't understand her, still, even if he did, she could not dissuade him. He'd gotten word from Minty that tonight was the night to carry out the plan they devised a month ago. He trusted Minty. He was determined to be free.

Frantically, Clarinda ran out of the barn. She ran to the main house, up onto the porch, and pounded on the front door. A minute later, she could see light oozing out from under the door. Then it opened. Standing there was Ira Booker, Massa Gethen's personal valet. He stood in his nightgown, holding a lamp, which he held out to light up Clarinda's face.

"Girl, what'cha doin' knockin' on folk's doors this time of night?"

"I gotta speak with the Massa."

"Are ya crazy? I wake the Massa this time of night, he'd put a bullet between my eyes. I wouldn't blame him, either. Besides, who ya think ya is, the Queen of Sheba. 'I wants to talk with the Massa'," he said, mockingly. "Besides, ain't ya suppose to be in the barn, doin' what comes natural?"

"I was, only the savage is tryin' to escape!"

"That ain't none of my business. Ya need to go to where the overseers stay. Ya know which shack is Hackett's?"

"Yea, I do."

"Then go knock on his door. He's the one ya need to tell. Stupid Girl…!" Ira declared, shutting the door in her face, not too hard as not to wake up the house.

Clarinda ran down the hill to where the overseers stayed. There were bunkhouses and one small shack where Hackett lived. She ran up on the porch, slamming her fist on the door. A light went on in the shack, a moment later the door opened. Except for not wearing his boots, he stood fully clothed. His hair stood up on edge.

"Girl, what'cha doin' here, ain't ya suppose to be at the barn?"

"It's the savage. He done got himself a file and he's cuttin' through his chains."

Leaving the door open, Hackett ran back in the shack. He sat down in the only chair, trying to put his boots on. He was having a hard time, bending over, his large gut got in the way.

"Girl, get in here and help me put my boots on."

Clarinda straddled his right leg, then his left, finally getting his boots on.

Hackett strapped on his gun and holster, taking down his Winchester rifle from off the wall. He ran out the door, followed by Clarinda.

At the barn door, Hackett stopped dead in his tracks. He turned to Clarinda, placing his finger against his lips, warning her to be quiet. He slowly opened the barn door. The wood creaked, getting louder with ever inch opened. He stopped, slipping through the opening.

The lamp was still lit, he could see everything clearly. Kujenga was nowhere to be found. On the ground where he usually stayed was a long length of chain with a link missing.

"Damn!" exclaimed Hackett.

Suddenly, the barn door slammed into him, knocking him to the ground. Before he could say a word, Kujenga was on him, picking him up by his collar as one might do to a disobedient child. Kujenga slammed him into the barn door, pressing him against it, placing the end of the metal file against his throat.

When the eyes of the two men met, fear flooded Hackett. He realized the hatred Kujenga held for him, that with one quick push of the file he'd be a dead man. He tried to struggle; Kujenga pressed the file into his throat. A droplet of blood trickled down his neck. Hackett felt the power in Kujenga's arms. He stopped his struggling, knowing he was no match for this angry slave.

Holding Hackett against the barn door with one arm, the one that held the file, with his other Kujenga took hold of his rifle. He loosed Hackett's holster, putting it over his shoulder.

There was no doubt in Hackett's mind this slave wanted him dead, and could easily do it. Yet, for some reason, he backed away, letting Hackett fall to the ground. Kujenga swung the barn door open wide, stepped out and started running north.

While all this was happening, Clarinda was in a panic. Standing in front of the main house, she screamed at the top of her lungs.

The front door of the main house opened. Ira flew out onto the porch, carrying his lamp.

"Damn it, girl, damn it," he shouted at her.

The next moment, all the lights in the main house were on. Furcas Gethen came running out, wearing his nightgown, a six-gun in his right hand, waving it in the air.

"What in Sam Hill is going on? Ira, what's this all about?"

Just then, Hackett came out of the barn. He held his throat, his fingers bloody, as well as the front of his shirt. Kujenga hadn't given him a mortal blow with the file, but he made his mark.

"Mr. Gethen," Hackett shouted. "The savage is loose."

"How the hell did that happen?"

"Someone snuck him a file."

"Did you do that?" Gethen growled at Clarinda.

The girl never stopped screaming this entire time. When Gethen shouted at her, it was all too much for her to bear. She fell in a dead faint.

"Ira, get her out of here."

The madam of the house showed up on the porch. "Furcas, what's going on?"

"Get back inside with the children. It's nothing. We've got a runaway slave. I'll take care of it."

"Is it the savage?" she called out.

"I said that I'd handle it. Now, go back inside," he shouted in anger. He pointed at Hackett. "Wake the others, leave a skeleton crew, we're going after him."

¤¤*

Word of what happened traveled through the compound like wildfire. Still, life goes on. All of us started our day like any other day, many off to the fields to work, Mama and I to the main house kitchen to prepare breakfast.

From the kitchen window, I saw Gethen and his men on horseback galloping across the fields into the forest.

I looked to the woods, wondering where Kujenga could be. I looked to the sky, saying a prayer.

Twenty-Six

I Do Not Know This Animal

There was no word of Treven Gilley. No one knew where he came from or where he went to. He was the first person Gethen thought about before going after Kujenga. However, with no way of contacting Gilley, Gethen looked to the next best thing. Sure, Charley One Horse failed the last time, but he was still a better tracker than Hackett or any of the other overseers. So, word was sent to Greg Sherman, who jumped at the chance to make a little extra money. Only, this time Gethen made a different agreement. If Charley One Horse couldn't track him down, Gethen would still have to pay for his time, except it would be for half the price agreed on. Both parties felt this to be fair.

One Horse did his usual inspection of the plantation only to come up with what everyone already knew. Kujenga was in the forest, heading north.

They hoped they could catch up with Kujenga on the first day, since they were on horseback. But he eluded them, going far into the woods, areas so rocky and thick with foliage they had to abandon their horses. Hackett left one of the men with the horses and most of their supplies by a small stream.

They moved forward till late in the afternoon. Finally, they decided to trek back to the horses, camp by the stream for the night, and then start fresh in the morning.

Once settled in for the night, they lay around the campfire, falling asleep one by one. It was then Gethen moved over next to Charley One Horse, determined to let him know of his displeasure with not getting his money's worth.

"So, what's your problem," Gethen asked. "He got away from you the first time, now; it looks like he's doing it, again."

"Oh, I'll get him," One Horse replied. "I need to change the way I hunt this man. He is different from most."

"Different? What do you mean by *different*…in what way?" Gethen sounded sarcastic in his question.

"I have hunted all colors of men, white, black, red, slave and free. Man is an animal. You must hunt him like one. Some are like wolves, some like horses, and others like eagles. This man is different. He understands the forest. He knows how to move about without disturbing it, without leaving his mark on it. He is not like any animal I know. I suspect it is something he learned in his homeland from his people, where the animals are different. I will catch him once I know how he thinks, once I know what kind of animal he moves like."

"And how will you do that?" Gethen asked.

"By forgetting, learning anew. Don't think of him as I have the others. All will be revealed. I must be open to Manitou, the Great Spirit, he will tell me."

Gethen just laughed. "You're a fool...a superstitious fool. I should send you back now, and quit wasting my money."

"If I do not catch him, I will pay Mr. Sherman, not you."

Charley One Horse rose to his feet, walking away from the campfire.

"Where are you going?" Gethen asked.

"I go to pray to the Great Spirit for guidance."

Gethen chuckled to himself, turning over on his side, closing his eyes.

"Idiots...I'm surrounded by idiots," he murmured to himself.

||*|*|*|*|*|*|*|*

Charley One Horse was born and raised Cheyenne, for the early part of his life, that is.

Years before Charley was born, the French forced the Cheyenne west to live on the open plains. Originally farmers, they now became hunters, learning to track the animals they hunted, the bison, eagle, deer, wolf, and many more. This was how Charley learned his tracking skills.

His people were nomads, roaming the Black Hills, living in teepees. From the beginning, the Cheyenne and the white man seldom saw eye to eye. It was the Cheyenne who fought the hardest against the white man. Perhaps for this reason, the white man came down hardest on the Cheyenne.

Battles and massacres decreased their numbers. They attacked Charley's village, taking prisoners. At first, the white man considered putting them into slavery, to labor alongside the black man. Though, when it was believed the red man couldn't be trusted, they abandoned the idea, and the slaughter of many began.

Still being quite young, they considered Charley not to be a lost cause. He was sent to Fort Laramie, Wyoming. There, his tracking skills were used by the cavalry. Tired of the fight, he learned the white man's ways and language.

After years of service, he left Fort Laramie, never telling anyone he was leaving. One day, he stole a horse, making his way to the southeastern part of the country. Through a series of unforeseen circumstances, he found employment on the Sherman Plantation as a tracker of animals for food, and on occasion, runaway slaves.

He tried keeping the traditions of his people in his life. But with each passing year it became more difficult as the memories faded. Only in prayer and in his dreams did he remember it well.

||*|*|*|*|*|*|*|*

In the morning, they started off, again, leaving one man to watch over the horses, and sending another back to the Plantation to fetch more supplies.

"I'm sending back for supplies, because I'm loosing faith in your abilities. I hope you still remember your promise to pay Sherman?" Gethen said.

Charley One horse ignored him, scouting out the terrain.

"So, what did the Great Spirit tell you last night?" again, Gethen's questioning was sour, filled with sarcasm.

"It is as I thought," One Horse replied. "This man was raised around animals I do not know, strange creatures from a strange land. Then I remembered hearing of a beast from where he comes from, an animal I have never seen. It is called a lion. That is why I found him hard to track. He is like a lion."

"And what's a lion like?" Gethen asked.

"They are strong and cunning, proud, and brave."

"So...?" Gethen laughed.

"So, a lion is just a big cat. I have hunted many kinds of cats. From here on, I will hunt him like a cat, just like the cougar. They like to be on high ground from their enemies. That means, we must go this way," One horse said, pointing off into the distance in the direction of Northwest.

"We'll see," Gethen murmured.

✳✳✳✳✳✳✳

All morning long, they moved slowly onward. Every so often, One Horse would stop to examine the surroundings. Almost midday, they came on a clearing. One Horse stopped, kneeling on the ground, inspecting.

"What is it?" Hackett asked, Gethen at his side, standing over One Horse.

Charley waved his hand over a spot of dry grass.

"We are catching up with him. He's slowing down." Charley thought for a moment. "I don't understand. Why is he slowing down?"

"He's gettin' tired," Hackett implied.

Charley shook his head. "No, this is a young, strong lion. He can move swiftly for many days. He is purposely slowing down." Charley stood up, addressing Hackett. "We are closing in on him. Tell your men to be careful, keep watch. He has a pistol and rifle."

Hackett laughed, "That savage wouldn't know what to do with them."

"I'm not saying he is a crack shot," Charley replied. "But he has seen how guns work. This is a man who has hunted with spear and arrow. He has good aim. I wouldn't laugh at him, if I were you. I'd keep watch."

Late in the afternoon, One Horse stopped again, kneeling on the ground.

"This is all wrong," he said to Hackett. "He is still slowing down. It is as if he wants us to catch up with him."

"You're talking nonsense. He's just getting tired," Gethen inferred.

"We stop here for the night," One Horse announced. "It will be dark soon. We can go no farther. We shouldn't go back to camp. We are too close to him to risk loosing him. We can continue with the morning light."

Gethen wanted to protest. He wanted to keep going till dark. "We've still got an hour of light. We don't want him to get another long lead on us."

"He won't get far," One Horse concluded. "He's not going to let that happen. He's playing with us, the way a lion plays with his prey."

||*|*|*|*|*

"Where the hell's my gun?" one of the overseers shouted, jumping to his feet.

"What are ya sayin'?" Hackett asked, Gethen and Charley One Horse by his side.

"Before I went to sleep, I took off my holster. I laid it down next to me, real close like. Now it's gone."

"Now he has a rifle, two pistols, and extra ammo," One Horse stated.

Without warning, Gethen hit the overseer hard with the back of his hand. The man went down hard, coming up with a bloody lip. Gethen took a silver coin from his pocket, tossing it down at him.

"Here's your month's wages. Go back to the Plantation, collect your things, you're fired."

The man didn't say a word. He rose to his feet, picking up his bedroll.

"That's not your bedroll. It's mine. Leave it, and get out of my sight," Gethen ordered.

The man did as he was told.

In less than five minutes, they broke camp and were on their way. Charley One Horse walked in front, moving slowly, inspecting the ground every few yards.

"These tracks are fresh. We're right on his trail," One Horse told Gethen and Hackett.

When they got to the summit of a high hill, One Horse stopped them.

"This makes no sense."

"What is it?" Hackett asked.

One Horse sounded bewildered, "He's turning around. He's heading back to the plantation."

"You're crazy. Why would he do that?"

"It's true. Look, see his tracks. He's heading back."

One Horse took up the pace, again. This time it was faster. He stopped now and then, checking the signs, shaking his head. At the bottom of the hill, they moved back into the depths of the forest. One Horse raised his hand to halt the group.

"Mr. Gethen, will you please come here?"

"What do you want?" Gethen asked, stepping forward.

"I apologize, Mr. Gethen. I cannot continue. I will honor my statement of yesterday. I will pay the fee to Mr. Sherman. I'm sorry, I can't go on."

"What are you trying to pull, One Horse?"

One Horse pointed to the ground. "Look, see his tracks. He is not only heading back to the plantation, he's making sure we know it. He made these track on purpose. He wants us to follow him."

"So...?"

"Understand, Mr. Gethen. I'm a fine tracker because I know how an animal will act and react. I do not know this animal. The most dangerous thing in a hunt is either a wounded animal or one that is unpredictable. This animal is both. From the looks of his tracks, he is limping. The pain is growing stronger with each mile. As well, he is very unpredictable. This is a very dangerous animal. I want nothing to do with it. I'm leaving."

Just then, a shot rang out. Everyone hit the ground.

"He's firing at us," Hackett hollered.

For a long moment, nothing happened, and then another shot blast echoed through the forest, ricocheting off the rocks Gethen was hiding behind, missing his head by only a few inches. Then another shot, then another.

Hackett moved into position behind a large rock. He saw gun smoke drifting out of a bush some twenty yards away. He took aim, held his breath, waiting. When another shot came from the bush, Hackett aimed directly at the puff of smoke and fired. A man screamed, followed by the thud of a body hitting the ground.

Hackett ran to the bush, looking behind it.

"Did you get him?" Gethen shouted.

There was no answer from Hackett. He remained silently staring at the ground behind the bush.

Gethen ran to him, along with Charley One Horse, followed by the others. Looking over Hackett's shoulder they saw, there on the ground, the dead body of the man Gethen had fired that morning.

Gethen bent low, recovering the silver coin from the vest-pocket of the dead man. Then Gethen took the rifle from the man's hand, pointing it at Charley One Horse.

"I made a deal, and I expect you to keep it. Now, you get back to tracking or I swear I'll leave you dead right here next to this son-of-a-bitch."

One Horse knew there was nothing to do other than comply. He walked back to where they once stood, taking up the tracks, once more.

Still staring down at the dead body, Hackett shouted to Gethen, "Shouldn't we bury him?"

"Let him rot," Gethen called back over his shoulder.

Twenty-Seven

Jealousy and Anger

I must tread on this ground lightly. In all my years, I don't know of a crueler, sadder, story.

First, understand what marriage meant to the slave. It was based on love and trust, as all marriages should be. However, a sword always hung over the head of the slave marriage. In your heart, it is permanent. Yet, in the real world, a husband could be sold, leaving his wife, and visa versa. As well, many parents and children were separated.

For some, this heavy weight of possible separation forced the slave to rethink their commitment to one another, many taking it lightly, if only for the sake of their ability to cope.

Still, many took their vows seriously, never thinking or acting as if it could all be taken away in the blink of an eye, at the whim of the person or persons who owned you.

It goes without saying, the differences in men and women made them see their commitment differently.

A man pursues a woman outside of his marriage for many different reasons, pleasure, conquest, and so on. It's a long list, yet, if you examine it closely, you seldom find matters of the heart involved in his actions. Men seldom stray looking for love and if so it is always temporary.

Women, for the most part, are led by the heart. For a woman to leave her husband for another man, it is usually because where they are coming from is a bad place and they are moving toward something they believe is good. Love and the heart are involved, and it is forever.

For this reason, sadly, a cheating husband was often tolerated, where as a cheating wife was looked down on. A man would even be lifted up by his fellow men. A woman would be scorned, even by her peers.

This is the way Albert saw the world. He never thought twice about cheating on his wife, Prudence. It was just part of life, the way things were, what was expected of him.

Nevertheless, God forbid, Prudence so much as looked at another man, Albert would have her hide and the man she was with.

I find it strange that a man who catches his woman with another man feels justified in killing him. A murder committed by a man who didn't think twice about committing the same act of adultery with *another* man's woman. It was all a vicious circle, if you ask me.

It also strikes me funny, how women will talk bad about a man who cheats. Yet, these are the same women, when given a chance, will take this so called *lowdown man* into her bed. I mean, who do you think these married men cheat with? You! It's just another vicious circle, only going in the opposite direction.

For all appearances, Prudence and Albert had a fine marriage. They were married for six years. They had two fine children, one six and one four, a boy and a girl, respectively. The shack they lived in was no better or worse than anyone else's shack. They both worked the fields, seldom having run-ins with the overseers. They were good neighbors; everyone liked them. Albert rarely drank and hardly ever strayed. When he did, Prudence turned a blind eye. She, herself, never considered anyone else other than Albert, was hardworking, true-blue, a good mother and wife.

Word traveled around the compound about how the Massa ordered all young slave women, married or not, to take turns spending nights in the barn, in hopes of birthing children by the savage.

This sent pandemonium through the compound. It angered everyone to be treated like cattle. The young women felt defiled. Their parents were heartbroken, having to see their daughters polluted in such a manner. But, the men were outraged, even those without a wife or woman. As far as they were concerned, these were their women, they belonged to them, not to any savage. They believed strongly and fully no one had the right to give away their women.

There was talk among the young men of a revolt, an actual taking up of arms, and fighting back, even if it was with only knives and farm tools. Nevertheless, everyone remembered what happened to Kendal Morris when he tried to revolt, taking up arms to defend his beloved Dolly. It was a losing battle that no one wanted to fight. There was nothing else to do other than grit your teeth and bear it.

Rumor was the savage pined for Audean, who had already conceived a baby girl by him. He would not sleep with any other woman save for Audean. This was a comfort to the men, yet, it brought up new problems. Keeping this in mind that the savage would stay true to Audean, all the husbands on the compound did everything they could to impregnate their wives, sometimes staying with them two to three times a day. Albert was no exception, nor was he immune to fits of jealousy and anger.

Albert prepared himself for when Prudence was to spend the night in the barn with the savage the only way he knew how. He made arrangements for the children to stay with neighbors; get his hands on some whiskey, and start to drink the minute he got home from the day's work. As drunk as he was, he was unable to sleep. Folks in nearby shacks were unable to sleep as well, as his drunken shouts of anger kept them awake.

The next morning when Prudence returned, he couldn't look at her or speak with her. In fact, after that night they rarely spoke a word to each other.

Albert couldn't stop thinking about it. When Prudence turned up in the family way, he did his best to convince himself the child was his, except he could only do it for so long. Finally, he gave into his suspicions. He spent most of his days drunk and withdrawn.

One morning just before sunrise, the entire compound was wakened by shouts coming from the shack of Albert and Prudence. It was the screams of their children. Folks stood outside the shack, arguing if they should force their way in to see what the problem was.

"At least knock on the door," someone declared.

However, all such talk was too late, a handful of overseers showed up to investigate the disturbance. They rushed the front door of the shack, breaking it down.

Inside, it was quick to see what happened. The children were huddled in the corner of the front room, crying. Standing in the center of the room was Albert, holding a log of wood in both hands. His face was contorted with anguish. There at his feet, was Prudence, bloody and dead.

The overseers drew their guns on him. It was too late, Albert had turned that corner. He'd completely lost his mind.

Wheeling the log over his head, he rushed toward the overseers. They had no choice but to fire. Albert took three shots in the chest. The log dropped from his hand, as he fell backwards, landing atop of Prudence.

It was damn a shame, and I'll never forget it till the day I die.

The two children were raised by their grandparents.

Twenty-Eight

As Quietly As We Could

Kujenga kept looking back, keeping an eye on his pursuers. He couldn't believe how slow and stupid they were. He purposely left obvious tracks. From afar, he did notice that the one with the red skin and the long hair knew what he was doing. The others were clueless.

More than once he stopped; breaking a few branches, also digging in his heals to leave a deeper track.

His foot, though better than it was, was not completely healed. Each mile, it hurt more, eventually swelling. He limped more than usual, which slowed him down.

Finally, he came to the creek where they camped a day ago. The horses were there, guarded by two of Gethen's men.

The two men sat on the ground, resting against the pile of saddles they'd relieved the horses of. They'd tied the horses near the stream; close enough so they could get a drink while they grazed on what little grass there was.

The sound of the rushing water covered up any sound Kujenga might make. He moved about freely, circling the camp. He thought of what mischief he could do, or if he should pass on by. He decided on mischief.

By the stream he untied the horses. They remained where they were, not moving. Kujenga moved silently into the center of the camp. The two men were either asleep or near-asleep, resting against the saddles, hats down over their eyes; arms crossed their chests, their legs crossed below.

Taking his rifle, Kujenga poked one of the men. He didn't stir, obviously in deep sleep. Kujenga poked the other man. All it did was make him snort, turning slightly to another direction. Then, using the tip of his rifle, Kujenga lifted the hat from the eyes of the man sleeping. The man woke with a jolt. Before he could move, Kujenga pressed the rifle tip into his nose. He remained motionless; his eyes wide and crossed looking down the muzzle of the gun. He reached over, waking the man sleeping on his side.

"Brett, wake up, we got visitors."

Brett opened his eyes wide, sitting up. Before they could do anything, Kujenga backed up, getting a good aim on both of them.

"Do ya think he knows how to use that?" Brett asked.

"I don't know, but I ain't gonna try to find out."

Kujenga pointed the rifle in the air, firing two shots. The horses went into a panic, running away, surely to get back to the safety of the plantation. Kujenga took their side arms out of their holsters from off the ground, tossing them yards away into the forest. Then, he backed away slowly. When he was at the edge of the camp, he turned running, disappearing into the deep woods.

The two men were clueless. Should they run after the savage, go after the horses, look for their guns, look for the hunting party, or go back to the plantation. They decided to look for their guns, and then wait at the camp for the others.

****

The shots echoed off the high hills and through the valley. The two shots sounded like a hail of bullets.

Everyone stopped in their tracks.

"What the hell is that?" Hackett asked.

"Gunshots," Charley One Horse answered.

"Sounds like an army," Hackett said.

"No, it's just the echoes. It was only two shots," One Horse replied. "It came from the camp. We need to get back right away."

"Hold on," Gethen said. "Which way are the tracks going?"

One Horse pointed ahead of them. "They lead in the same direction as the camp."

"Very well, we'll go to the camp. Only, we need to split up, so we can surround the camp. There's no reason to come in all at once, having him pick us off one by one. Half of us will follow One Horse. Hackett, you take half the men, go left, circling around."

"I want ya, ya, and ya to come with me," Hackett ordered, pointing to the men he wanted.

Both parties began running as fast as the terrain let them.

****

At the camp, the two men were looking for their weapons.

"He threw them somewhere around here," remarked Brett.

"The hell with it, it's getting' dark. We'll never find them."

"Wait one second," Brett said, bending down. "Here they are."

When they walked back to the center of camp, putting on their holsters and putting their guns in them, they discussed their dilemma.

"We're dead men, Sam; ya know that, don't ya?" Brett sighed. "Surely Gethen heard the gunshots. When he gets here, we're gonna have to do some explainin'.'"

"I got an idea," said Sam. "Give me ya knife."

"What for..?"

"Just give it to me."

Sam took the knife.

"Now, give me ya hand."

"My hand, what the hell for...?"

Sam took hold of Brett's hand, running the blade across his palm.

"What are ya crazy?" shouted Brett.

Sam took the blade, slicing his own palm.

"Great, now we're both bleedin'," complained Brett.

"Listen," said Sam. "When they get here, tell 'em two shots were fired. The savage shot once, missin' us. Then I shot, hit him, he ran off, wounded."

"Why can't I say I shot 'em"

"Because it's my idea...now, come on, let's run this way. Make sure ya get blood on plenty of rocks and trees. They'll think he ran off in this direction. At least they won't find out we was asleep; they'll think we was wide awake doin' our best. Just make sure no one sees your hand, when they get here."

They ran about a third of a mile uphill, going north. Then they turned around, going back to the camp.

It was so dark when they got back to the camp, they lit a fire. As soon as the flames grew high enough to see, out jumped the other men from the hunting party. They came from all directions, with their guns drawn.

"Hold on, don't shoot," Sam shouted, careful not to raise his palm to them.

Gethen stepped forward. "All right, what happened?"

Sam told the story of the two shots fired, and how he wounded the savage who got away, running north.

Charley One Horse walked to the edge of the camp, bent low, running his fingers over a large rock. One Horse came back to stand with Gethen and Hackett.

"He's right," One Horse said. "Look here, blood." Then something dawned on One Horse. "It don't make no sense. Why would he make sure to lead us this way, and then head back up hill, going north?"

"I don't care why or what he's doing. Can you track him," Gethen asked.

"Of course," One Horse said. "A blood trail is the easiest to follow. We'll just have to wait till morning."

"No," Gethen shouted. 'We continue, this minute, right now."

"How do you expect to follow a blood trail in the dark?" One Horse remarked.

Gethen looked to Hackett, "Get the men to make some torches." He turned to One Horse. "We hunt the savage, tonight."

****

Kujenga headed south, toward the plantation. He hoped that without their horses the hunting party would move slower giving him enough time to do what he wanted to do.

At the last of the high summits, he looked to the horizon. He saw the plantation off in the distance. The thought of seeing the woman he loved and his daughter allowed him to ignore the pain in his swollen foot. He now moved faster and with purpose.

When he got to the edge of the forest, it was sunset. Hiding behind a rock, he looked across the fields to where the workers were finishing for the day. By sundown, they'd left the fields for their homes.

Mother and I were just finishing in the main house kitchen. It was such a difficult day to get through, worrying about Kujenga, not knowing where he was or what happened to him.

After we cleaned up, we left for home. Mama went on ahead, while I picked up Nzuri at the home of one of the older women in the slave quarters. Walking across the compound with my baby in my arms, I felt so close to her, holding her tightly. What would be her future? Overcome with emotion, I had to stop twice to collect myself.

At home, I found Papa sitting on the porch.

"Here, let me have her," Papa said, holding out his arms. I placed Nzuri in them. "Ya go in and help your mother. Tell her not to make anything for me. I'm not hungry, tonight."

The four of us, Mama, Deidra, Lucius, and me, sat at the table, picking at our food. It seemed no one had an appetite.

When I tried to help Mama clean up, she stopped me.

"No, I'll take care of this. Ya go nurse my grandbaby and put her to bed."

I walked out on the porch to find Papa holding Nzuri close to his chest, rocking her. His head was down, looking at her, not even looking up when I stepped out to the porch.

"Papa, are ya cryin'?"

"Me, no, I'm just tired."

"I need to nurse her and put her to bed, Papa."

Without a word, he handed her over.

"I love ya both," I heard him say, as I entered the house.

I went into the bedroom, closing the door behind. Deidra and Lucius both knew better than to come in while I was nursing Nzuri. I was alone in the dark, sitting on the edge of my bed, my child at my breast, looking out the window at the darkness of the night.

At first I thought my eyes were playing tricks on me. Looking to the trees a few yards from the house, I could have swore I saw someone move from behind one tree to another. Looking again, I realized I had. Whoever they were, they came out of hiding, starting for the house. As he approached, I got a good look. It was Kujenga. I buttoned my blouse;

put the baby in the center of the bed, between two pillows. I rushed to the window, dropping to my knees. He ran to the window. The next instant, we were kissing.

"Kujenga, why are ya here? Ya need to go. You'll get ya'self killed."

"Love Audean...Love Nzuri," was all he knew how to say, and all he needed to say.

I could hear the others moving about the house, I became frightened.

"Kujenga, ya need to go hide, come back later."

Not knowing what I was saying, he looked at me, confused.

"Mama, Papa, ya go hide. Come back later when they're asleep."

I pointed to the door as I said this, and then tilting my head, placing my hands on the side of my head, mimicking someone sleeping.

He instantly understood, backing away from the window.

"Come back when they're asleep," I repeated, again, tilting my head, my hands resting against my cheek.

He ran off behind the bushes to hide.

"Are ya all right in there?" Mama asked through the door, worrying why I was taking such a long time.

I looked, Nzuri was fast asleep.

****

Hours later in the night when all was quiet, I looked to see if my brother and sister were asleep, they were. Nzuri was asleep in her small cradle that Papa made for her.

Again, I went to the window, falling to my knees. When he saw me, leaving his guns behind, Kujenga came out from behind the trees, silently to my window. We kissed long and deep. Then he began to work his way in through the window. I knew it was foolishness, but I wanted so desperately to hold him.

We stood at the window in each others arms, kissing. Then he moved away from me, walking to the cradle. He bent low, kissing his daughter on her forehead. The child cooed softly. He turned, taking me again in his arms.

As quietly as we could, we lowered ourselves onto my bed. I was lost in his arms. I wanted to disappear into him, to hide in him. I didn't know what the morning would bring. I feared thinking about it. I couldn't see any way we could be together. If we never saw each other again, at least, we would have that night.

Careful not to wake the others, gently, softly, we made love.

Afterwards, he rested in my arms like a big child. I was so full of joy at that moment. I never wanted it to end; still, I knew it would.

I looked across the room. In what little light coming in through the window, I saw Deidra smiling at me from her bed.

Go to sleep, I silently mouthed to her. Still smiling, she rolled over.

Twenty-Nine

Checkmate

We'd both fallen asleep. I woke up in his arms. Looking out the window, it relieved me to see it was still dark.

"Kujenga," I whispered.

He stirred slowly, opening his eyes, kissing me once more before getting out of bed. I got out of bed, also. He bent low, kissing his sleeping daughter. Standing at the opened window, he did his best to convey his plan.

"Audean...Nzuri....Kujenga," he said, holding up three fingers representing us. "Kujenga..." he said pointing to one of the three fingers. He took hold of that finger with his other hand, and then moved that hand away from the two remaining fingers. He was clearing stating that he was going away. "Kujenga..." he said, holding a finger up, away from the other two. Then, he moved that finger back, next to the other two. With the three fingers back together, "Audean...Nzuri...Kujenga." Telling me we would be back together sometime in the future. He moved the three away from him. In pantomime, he conveyed that he was to go away, but he'd be back to take us with him.

"No, Kujenga. Ya shouldn't even be here now. Ya must go away before they catch ya. Never come back here, for any reason."

He looked at me, confused.

I held up one finger, "Kujenga," I said, moving it away from the two fingers I held up in my other hand. "Go away...never come back."

I believe he understood what I tried to say.

"Audean....Nzuri...Love," he said.

"I know. We love ya, too, but ya gotta go. Don't ever come back," I said, pushing him away, toward the window. He tried to kiss me, but I pushed him backwards. "No...no," I said, hitting him in the chest. Finally, when it seemed all my efforts to sway him to never return was hopeless, I slapped his face. "Go away," I nearly shouted.

He was not that easily deceived. He knew I loved him. Nothing in the world could stop him from returning for his family. He kissed me once more. With a smile on his face, he hopped out the window. I watched him rush to the bushes to recover his guns. He silently stole back into the dark.

****

Charley One Horse walked in front of the others, moving his torch back and forth along the ground.

"Gethen, come here, please," he called out.

Gethen who was only a few feet behind came forward.

"Look at this," One Horse said, shining his torch on the side of a rock.

"It's blood. What about it?" Gethen questioned.

One Horse moved a few feet in the opposite direction, illuminating the trunk of a tree.

"More blood, so…?" Gethen wondered.

"And here…?" One Horse said, holding his torch near another rock.

"Blood," Gethen announced.

"Two things," One Horse pointed out, "This man is bouncing from side to side, randomly. The only reason a man would bounce like that is if he were seriously wounded. If he were hurt that bad, we'd find him dead, already. Now, here we are a quarter mile from camp, not only is there no body, but there isn't anymore blood. The trail stops here."

"Hackett," Gethen shouted.

"Yes, sir…"

"Bring me those two idiots."

Brett and Sam stood before Gethen.

"What are you two trying to pull?"

"We're not tryin' to pull anything, boss. He shot at us, I shot him, and this is the direction he ran in."

Gethen knew something was wrong, but he couldn't' say what. He looked to Charley One Horse. "What do you suggest we do?"

"I say we head back to the plantation. That was where he was headed. I think that's where he's going."

Gethen turned, pushing his way through the men. "Hackett…we head back to the plantation."

****

If you could look down on it all from heaven, it would have looked like a chess game only a few moves from checkmate. Gethen, Hackett, Charley One Horse, and the others, were making their way through the forest, back to the plantation. Momma and I were in the main house kitchen, preparing breakfast for the Gethen family. Papa and the other slaves, along with the overseers were out working in the fields. Nzuri was with the elderly women of the slave quarters. And Kujenga…he was the loose cannon. No one knew where he was.

All heads turned, everyone stopped working, to see Gethen's hunting party emerge from the woods, starting across the fields. Immediately, what was obvious was they hadn't captured the runaway. They moved across the fields slow, tired, dirty, hungry, and apparently crushed.

Looking out the back window, Mama and I saw it all.

The overseers whipped a few of the slaves to get their focus back on their work.

Gethen walked in front of the group, followed by Charley One Horse and Hackett. As they made their way across a newly plowed field, through the furrows of dirt, a gunshot rang out, shattering the air. A puff of smoke flew up from the dirt a few feet in front of Gethen.

Everyone hit the ground, Gethen, the hunting party, even the slaves and the overseers. All was quiet, save for the sound of the wind across the land and the caw of a few blackbirds circling overhead.

"Did anyone see where that shot came from?" Gethen said, still on his belly, as were the others.

"No, sir," Hackett responded.

A long time passed without incident'

"Well, damn, we can't just stay on the ground all-day," Gethen said, standing, pulling his gun from his holster.

Slowly, everyone stood up, including the slaves and the overseers. No one moved, no one spoke, and they all knew they weren't safe. Savage or not, a bullet in the head is as bad as one from a marksman.

In the next instant, another shot blasted through the air, sending up a gust at Gethen's feet. This time he didn't fall to the ground, his gun held tightly in his hand, running forward. The others followed. In fear, the slaves remained huddled on the ground.

Surprisingly, Gethen and his men weren't shot at. They made it across the field safely, onto the main thoroughfare of the plantation. They were in the slave quarters.

Gethen's largest concern was his family. "We need to get to the main house," he shouted to his men.

Not knowing where the gunman was, they hid behind the shacks in the slave compound, running from one shack to the next until they were on the edge of the quarters.

The main house was not far off in the distance, nevertheless, a gunman made the distance a world away, for between the slave quarters and the main house was nothing but open space. Anyone crossing it would be an easy target, easy to hit.

Without warning, a shot hit the side of one of the shacks, sending dry splinters in all directions. There was a small cloud of gun smoke rising above the main house.

"He's on the roof!" Hackett shouted. He pointed to some of his men. "I'm gonna try to rush him. Cover me."

They peered from behind the shacks, rifles drawn; they began firing at the roof. Gun in hand, Hackett, scurried to a small bush halfway between the compound and the main house. Keeping to the ground, he fired his pistol.

Another gunshot came from the roof. Kujenga was on the other side of the roof, shooting over the top. As soon as he fired, the men sent a hail of bullets at the roof. Hackett jumped up, running. Others came out of hiding and began rushing the house, constantly firing their guns.

Fearing for his family, even Gethen joined in on the attack.

As they approached, the potshots from the roof stopped. When they got to the house, they stopped shooting, as well.

"Quick, run around! Get him, before he gets down off the roof," Hackett ordered.

Four of the men ran counterclockwise around the building.

When Gethen made it to the house, he ran onto the porch and in through the front door. He ran from room to room. He found no one. Rushing into the kitchen, he found Mama and me hiding under the table.

"Where's my family?" he shouted.

"I don't know, sir, they might be upstairs," Mama cried.

The next second, he was out the kitchen door, taking the stairs going up two by two. He found no one in any of the children's bedrooms. He rushed to the master bedroom, kicking the door open. He saw no one. Then, there was the sound of crying coming from under the bed. He fell to his knees to see his family huddled, his wife clutching their two children close to her.

"It's all right," he whispered. "Just stay where you are. You're safe. I'll be back soon."

He rushed down the stairs and out of the building. "Did you find that son-of-a-bitch," he called to Hackett.

"Not yet, sir..."

Just then, the four men who'd ran to the back of the building came around from the other side.

"No sign of him, sir," said one of the men.

"That's impossible," Hackett declared. "Go round, again." He pointed to some of the other men. "Get the ladder on the side of the house, go up on the roof, and see if he's still there."

Everything became chaotic. There were men climbing the ladder, men on the roof, while others continued circling the house. There was no sign of Kujenga.

Gethen grabbed Hackett by the collar. "He must be in the house. That woman, his woman, she must be hiding him in the kitchen. Take some men to the kitchen. Don't kill him. I want to deal with that son-of-a-bitch, myself."

****

After Gethen rushed out of the kitchen and up the stairs, I realized the gunfire had stopped. I got up from under the table, and went to the back window to have a look.

"Don't go near the window," Mama warned me, but I was too worried for Kujenga to care. I saw four men running. After they passed the window, Kujenga jumped down off the roof.

"In here," I whispered, holding the door open.

He rushed inside. It was then I realized my mother had never as much as seen Kujenga. She rose from under the table. The two of them stared at each other for a moment, and then smiled.

The next moment we heard shouting outside, and footsteps above us as if someone was on the roof.

"Ya gotta leave," I said, pointing out the window across the fields to the forest.

There he was standing before me, rifle in hand with two pistols tucked in the waist of his pants. He smiled at me. I knew even if he understood my words, he would not heed them.

Suddenly, the kitchen door flew open. A man came rushing in, pistol in hand. Kujenga brought the butt of his rifle up, striking the man on his chin. He flew backwards into the kitchen door slamming it in the face of his companions. Kujenga put two shots through the door. They would think twice before opening it again.

"Go...!" I said.

Giving me one last smile, he turned, rushing out the backdoor.

****

The two shots coming from within the house caught everyone's attention.

"They must have got him," Hackett said to Gethen.

Just then, men came running out of the house, clearly frightened.

"He's held in the kitchen. I think he got Sam," said one of the men.

"Well, then rush him," Gethen ordered. "Some men go to the backdoor. I want you," he shouted at the men who'd come out of the house, "I want you to get back in there."

"Hold on," Charley One Horse said. "He's not in the kitchen." One Horse pointed a few yards away. "There he goes."

Sure enough, Kujenga was out in the open, running to of all places, to the barn. He opened the barn door, leaving it open, and rushed inside.

"Now, we've got him," Gethen said.

Thirty

The End of the Day

The barn door was wide open. It was pitch-black inside. Kujenga ran to the back of the barn into the darkness. They couldn't see him, but he could see them. They kept their distance. Being that far away, they couldn't get a good shot at him, even if they could see him.

"That is the only door. There are no windows. Now, we have him," Gethen said, smiling.

"Yeah, but how?" Hackett asked. "We can't rush him straight on. That barn door opening is so wide; he can see us from both angles."

"Two things," Gethen said to Hackett. "Go into the main house, upstairs you'll find my wife and children. Tell them they no longer have to hide; however, I want them to remain in the house. Then I want you to go to the kitchen, find that girl who had the savage's child. Bring her here."

The next thing I knew, I was standing next to Gethen, staring at the opening in the barn. Mama came out with me, to give me some support. No one paid her any mind, especially Gethen.

"Call him out," Gethen said. "Tell him, if he comes out now I'll spare his life."

"I can't," I said. "I don't speak his language."

He looked coldly into my eyes. "Do your best," he growled.

"Kujenga…!" I shouted into the barn. There was no answer. "Kujenga…!" I shouted, again.

"Audean…!" Kujenga shouted from out of the dark.

"Kujenga, come out!" I said. Though he didn't understand me, the worry in my voice conveyed my message. I knew he would never come out. I also knew that now there was no way for him to escape. It was at that moment the realization hit me that I would lose him. There was no way he'd survive. He'd be dead before the end of the day.

"This is useless," Gethen snarled, pushing me aside. I went to the back of the crowd to stand with my mother.

Some of the slaves who'd been working nearby in the fields came over to have a look.

"Someone get them out of here," Hackett ordered.

"No," Gethen told Hackett. "Let them stay. I want them to see this."

I noticed my father was one of the slave spectators.

"Well, don't just stand there, do something," Gethen demanded, looking directly at Hackett.

"Ya two," Hackett said, pointing at the men. "One of ya come at him from the right, the other come at him from the left."

The men split into two directions, one going far left, the other far right. They moved slowly in on the barn, except the angle wasn't wide enough. Kujenga shot at both of them. The first shot missed the man on the left, still it was close. The man backed away in fear. The other shot caught the other man on his foot. In a flash, the tip of his boot exploded, a geyser of blood shot up, the man fell to the ground. Another man rushed out, grabbing the back of his collar, dragging him out of range and to safety.

I was so frightened, falling into my mother's arms, quivering and crying.

They stood waiting and watching for hours. The sun began to sink low. Gethen and Hackett discussed scenarios, like two generals making battle plans.

Sunset colors smeared across the western horizon. In the east, the dark of night washed over the sky like an ebb tide. They had spent the day at a stand off.

"That's it, I've made a decision," Gethen announced. "Hackett, have your men go into the kitchen. There is a large five gallon can of kerosene. Have them douse the barn on all three sides. We'll smoke him out, or burn him alive. Whichever, I don't care."

Hackett went into action. After bringing back the can of kerosene from the kitchen, one of the men circled the barn. Starting at the back, he drenched the old wood of the barn, and then the sides. When he finished, abandoning the can, he circled around, coming back to the others.

All this time, Hackett had some of his men make up three torches. They lit one of them. "Go around back, set it on fire," Hackett ordered the man holding the lit torch.

"No, let me do it!" a voice cried from the group of on-watching slaves. Everyone turned to see who it was. A lone slave moved to the front of the others. It was my father.

"Let me do it. I won't even have to go around back. I'll throw that right through the front door."

Normally, Gethen would have a slave beaten within an inch of his life for being so insolent, speaking up without being spoken to. Only now, Gethen's curiosity got the best of him.

"And why would you want to do this?" Gethen asked.

"Because I hate this man," Papa replied. "He's ruined my daughter, my family, disrespecting me. I want him dead. All this time, I had to serve him his meals. Every night I watched him eat, wanting to kill him. I beg of you, let me do it."

Gethen smiled, nearly bursting into laughter. "Give him the torch. I'd like to see this."

Hackett took the torch from his man, giving it to Papa.

Papa stood out front of everyone, staring at the barn.

"Go ahead," Gethen chuckled. "He's all yours."

I was shaking. My arms tightened around my mother. I wanted to look away. I couldn't. For whatever strange reason, I turned around, looking at the main house. There, standing, watching, at the second floor window was Mrs. Gethen and her two children. Both children were crying.

Papa took in a deep breath. He was off running toward the barn. When he was a third of the way across the span, gunshots came from the darkness of the barn. The bullets hit the ground at my father's feet. Papa began to zigzag, always moving forward. The gunshots from the barn continued, each of them missing by inches.

When he was three quarters across the span, Papa stopped, pulling his arm back, then forward, he tossed the lit torch deep into the barn. The gunfire stopped. Papa turned around, running back to the others.

We could only image that Kujenga tried to stomp out the flames, although, with all that dry hay, it would be impossible.

First, we heard the crackling sound of the hay catching fire. Then there was a slight yellow glow within the darkness. This small glow began to grow until the inside of the barn was fully illuminated. We heard the whooshing sound of air being drawn into the building. Flames appeared on the outward walls, licking their way upwards. In no time, flames completely engulfed the barn.

I fell to my knees, crying. I felt my mother's hands trying to lift me. But, I couldn't move. I was fused to that spot by my tears.

Gethen looked at the barn in flames, he smiled. Still smiling, he turned to my father. "I suppose you expect thirty pieces of silver for your deed?" Gethen laughed when he realized his irony was lost on all those around him. He addressed Hackett as he pointed to the crowd of slaves. "I don't want any of them going to their homes until that barn is nothing but ashes. Do you understand?" He started for the main house. "I'm going to bed. I'm tired of all this."

Thirty-One

We Had a Plan

I believe it was the next morning. I wasn't sure. I didn't even remember when or how I got home. I woke up in my bed, my daughter sleeping beside me. The sun poured through the window on us, golden like honey.

Reflecting on my thoughts, it all seemed like a dream. A part of me didn't want to believe it was true. I knew if I dwelt on it, I'd start crying, again. I reached out, taking Nzuri in my arms. She cooed slightly.

"I will never let ya forget your father," I vowed to her.

The bedroom door opened. Mama stuck her head in.

"Ya up?" she asked. I turned to look at her. "Good. How do ya feel?"

I just sighed. She understood.

"Why don't ya come out for breakfast?"

"I don't feel very hungry," I said.

"Come out, anyways. Ya father and I want to talk to ya. Get dressed, first."

She slipped her head back out, closing the door.

Reluctantly, I got Nzuri and me ready for the day. In the kitchen, I found my parents sitting at the table.

"Where are Deidra and Lucius?" I asked.

"I've sent them out," Papa replied.

"Why aren't ya in the fields, Papa? And why ain't ya at the main house?" I asked Mama.

They both were acting so strange

"Sit down," Papa said.

I took a seat. They were silent for the longest time.

"We know how hard this has been on ya," Papa said.

"Ya helped kill him," I whispered, nearly in tears.

"I know how ya feel," he said. "That's why your mother and I have made a decision. You're to leave the plantation."

"Leave the plantation...how?"

"Don't worry about that, we've seen to a way."

"But...why?" I asked.

"It's best for all of us," Mama said.

"I don't want to leave. Where will I go?"

"It's all been arranged," Papa answered. "Now, get ya stuff ready."

I was in shock. I didn't know what to do besides obey.

Twenty minutes later, I stood before them, all of Nzuri's and my things in a single pillow case.

My parents stood up, heading for the door, clearly expecting me to follow.

"What about Deidra and Lucius?" I asked.

"We'll say your good-byes to them for ya. In time, they'll understand."

"I don't understand," I said.

They ignored me, leaving the shack. I followed closely.

We walked away from the slave quarters. Doing our best to avoid the fields where the others were working, we headed for the forest.

"Where are ya takin' us?" I asked.

"It'll be all right," Mama said.

In the forest, we continued walking. We walked for nearly an hour. Nzuri, usually a sweet natured child, began to fuse.

"Where are we goin'," I said in protest.

They ignored me, tramping onward. At the foot a high hill, we began to climb. I found the going difficult. Papa took Nzuri in his arms, so I was free to use both my arms to keep my balance.

Another hour later, we reached the summit. I looked back, seeing the plantation below. There was the compound where we lived; the fields where our people toiled, the main house where Mama and I worked. Lastly, there was the barn, now a pile of ashes with smoke still rising from it.

There was a rustle coming from the bushes. I watched as a small black women appeared guiding a donkey behind her. She stopped before me.

"My name is Minty. I've come to take ya away on the Underground Railroad."

I'd heard of such things, never sure if it was a rumor or a dream.

"I got a surprise for ya," she continued. "I don't want ya to be frightened."

I looked at her strangely. She turned, calling to one of the bushes.

"Njoo," she said.

I nearly fell to my knees, in shock. Kujenga walked out from behind the bush. I ran to his arms. It was a long time before we stopped kissing, and I looked to my parents and the old woman.

"I don't understand," I said in tears.

Papa walked over to us. To my surprise, instead of handing Nzuri to me, he handed her to Kujenga. Mama came over to stand by his side. They were smiling at us.

"I'm sorry I never told ya our plan," Papa said. "We just wanted to keep ya and Nzuri safe, in case things didn't work out."

Mama took hold of Papa by his arm.

"Ya mother and me knew how much in love ya two were. We decided to do something about it. We had a plan. Minty, here, was in on it, too. Every night when everyone thought I was waitin' in the barn for Kujenga to finish his supper, we was diggin' a tunnel. Well, not really a tunnel, more like a crawl space in the back of the barn. The plan was for Kujenga to escape; only later he'd get caught in the barn. We knew they'd burn down the barn. Kujenga was long gone before the fire ever started."

I didn't know what to do, be angry or thank them. All I could do was cry.

"Let me hold my grandbaby one more time before ya goes," Mama said, reaching out to Kujenga. Mama held Nzuri as Papa held them both.

"I hate to say it, but we gotta go," Minty announced. 'We got a lot of ground to cover before we get to the first safe house."

Reluctantly, Mama gave back Nzuri to me. She leaned forward, kissing my cheek.

"Ya take care, child," she whispered sorrowfully.

Papa looked into my eyes. "Promise me, the first chance ya get, the two of ya get married."

"Of course, Papa," I pledged.

"Ya take care of these two," he said to Kujenga.

"Yes," Kujenga said, instinctively understanding.

They backed away slowly.

"We love ya, child," Mama said, crying.

"I love ya both," I said.

"We love ya too, baby," Papa said.

Minty guided me forward. Kujenga helped me onto the donkey. We started down the hill. I looked back to see my parents waving good-bye. A little ways farther, I looked back, again. They were gone.

There we were, a strange group on the move, our guardian angel, Minty, out front guiding the way. The husband at the side of his wife and newborn child were on their way to the New Jerusalem.

EPILOGUE

It was so long ago, like a dream within a dream, told to me by someone else, or a book I read about the life of another. The pages now yellow from age. Being old is so strange. Not something you know, just something you think about. You feel it only when you move. It all goes by so quickly.

It's only right that I tell you what happened. You've come with me so far, I owe you at least that much.

We followed the Underground Railroad for weeks, until we got to Minty's farm in upstate New York. It was a small place, welcoming and warm.

We stayed there for nearly a year. Both Kujenga and I worked on the farm for our keep, though sometimes we worked for other folks, especially in the winter. Nzuri did what children do; she grew so much that first year.

Minty found us a home and work up in Canada. It was strange to leave the country. Canada was so similar, yet so different. It took awhile getting used to it.

I worked for June Estelle Hubert, cleaning house and cooking for her and her husband, Theodore. It was easy work, compared to my past work, and the pay was good. June Estelle and Theodore were wealthy, living in a large mansion. They were elderly, needing more care with each passing year. They were a sweet couple, and a joy to work for. I worked for them five years, until Theodore died. After that, June Estelle closed up the house, moving to Chicago to live with her sister.

As for Kujenga, he was not one to shy away from hard work. On Minty's farm, he dirtied his hands at everything from plowing, wood chopping, taking care of livestock, and bucking barley at another local farm.

In time, his English improved. Eventually, he was able to hold a conversation with the best of them. It's interesting to note, once he was able to communicate, the distance between him and the world, such as what he experienced on the plantation, disappeared. He was very well liked, and we made many friends.

Oh, we kept true to our pledge to my parents. Kujenga and I married.

When we moved to Canada, strangely, Kujenga took to speaking French like a fish to water. He became so fluent in French; some folks thought him born to the area.

Minty got him a job at a glassblowing factory, stoking the fire. It was hard work, paying very well. There was another of Minty's runaways working there. A fellow named Monroe. We became good friends with him and his family, a lifelong friendship.

Kujenga and I always wanted to have more children, but it was not to be. Nzuri was our only child, the love of our lives. She grew tall and beautiful. We saw to it she was well educated. Hopefully, she would not have to work as hard as her patents to make a living. As well, we did everything in our power for her to never know want or fear.

After years of working for others, saving our money, we decided to make a go on our own. We bought some property, erected a cabin, and started to raise cranberries. That's right, cranberries. Don't laugh. It turned out to be very profitable, a difficult crop to grow, seasonal, but well worth it.

More than once, I asked Kujenga if he missed the old country in Africa. It was so long and far away, now, it didn't enter his mind. He was so happy in his life; he said the past didn't matter. I understood what he meant, feeling the same.

I am old, now. I live with my daughter, Nzuri, her husband Clark, and my grandson, Peter, in Boston. Nzuri owns a typing service that she runs from their home, which is good; I have her to myself all-day long. Clark is a pharmacist. He's a good man, I like him very much. Peter is just finishing school. He is the smartest, most handsome boy in the world.

It's been many years since Kujenga passed on. Oh, don't feel sad. He had a long and happy life. He died a very old man. As for me, this old body refuses to give up the ghost. But, it won't be long, now. I'll see my Kujenga soon enough. I'll see my love, again. We'll be young, once more. Our spirits will fly to where we were the happiest, where the wild cranberries grow.

THE END

Michael Edwin Q. is available for book interviews and personal appearances. For more information contact:

Michael Edwin Q.
C/O Advantage Books
P.O. Box 160847
Altamonte Springs, FL 32716
michaeledwinq.com

Other Titles in this series buy Michael Edwin Q:

Born A Colored Girl: 978-1-59755-478-4
Pappy Moses' Peanut Plantation: 978-1-59755-482-8
But Have Not Love" 978-1-59755-494-7

To purchase additional copies of these book visit our bookstore website at:
www.advbookstore.com

Longwood, Florida, USA
"we bring dreams to life"™
www.advbookstore.com